SAIL ON SERENADE

JAKKI JELENE

Published by Doorway Publishing

ISBN: 978-1-954771-01-7

Cover Design: Jakki Jelene

Published in the United States of America

www.jakkijelene.com

"The fishermen know that the sea is dangerous and the storm terrible, but they have never found these dangers sufficient reason for remaining ashore."

– *Vincent van Gogh*

CHAPTER ONE

Noah Sullivan was aroused by the sweet smell of saltwater filling his nostrils. Sunlight teased him awake as it filtered through the tiny porthole next to his bed, which was snugly set at the bow of *The Serenade.* It was a fine late September morning and the white ship, a 38-foot sailboat he would call home for the next year, was bobbing gently in a marina in Portland, Maine. He had been at sea almost two full weeks but made very little headway in the time since leaving his hometown of Newland in northern Maine aboard the small vessel with his new friend and mentor, Conrad.

Conrad had offered to take Noah on his yearly travels south to the Florida Keys after teaching Noah to sail over the summer. Noah had employed Conrad after discovering an interest in sailing and acquiring a thirst for adventure after a lifetime of being relegated to the confinements of his childhood home, Birchwood Cottage. For the first seventeen years of his life, Noah had known little of the world and spent the better part of his years sheltered by his overanxious aunt after being left in her charge by his largely absent father. His mother died when he was still an infant and his father coped with her loss by pursuing his career as a fisherman off the coast of Maine full-time, which meant he was rarely home. After a time of personal development, Noah hoped to rekindle a relationship with his father before receiving word that he had been lost at sea. Between that devastating loss and his Aunt Prissy's recent marriage, he decided to go seek a little coastal adventure for himself and took Conrad up on his offer.

Noah didn't depart from his hometown completely unencumbered though. He left behind his heart in the very capable hands of his sweetheart, Lily. Noah credited Lily's friendship with much of his growth over the past year and she was also the one who encouraged him in his newfound dream to see a slice of the world. Separation was nothing new to them, as her family now resided in Boston, but they spent a glorious two months together that summer before parting and promised to put their love on hold while Noah set sail and Lily finished her schooling. While still so young, they spoke tentatively of marriage upon his return which wouldn't be for another nine months. But since *The Serenade's* next stop was in Boston, Noah was looking forward to spending a few days with his darling girl in the city before shipping off for the bulk of the trip.

For a few minutes longer, Noah laid in his bed recalling the moment he and Lily saw each other again after many months of separation following her family's move to Boston. Too many misunderstandings and tragedies had come between them, but all was put to rest the day her family returned to the blue cottage in Newland for their summer vacation. Noah had been painting on the terrace, as he often did, when he saw his beloved Lily traipsing down the beach in his direction. He jumped over the hedges that lined his yard and ran to greet her. The two met halfway on the sand and kissed away all the doubt and fear of the past. They confessed their love for one another and for the rest of the summer, were completely inseparable.

Noah thought on that first kiss often, though many were to follow. His toes still tingled with the memory of Lily's lips gently pressed to his. She was an enchanting creature, full of the love of life, child-like in her innocence, and deeply wise in her years. She had flipped his whole world upside down with her patience and unconditional love. He couldn't wait to see her again in the coming days but wondered how he was going to get through the next nine months following their final moments together in Boston.

He was still lost in his thoughts when Noah heard Conrad call out to him from the deck, "Hey Sleeping Beauty, rise and shine! We're about to get underway and should be outward bound by 0-900."

Noah was still getting used to all the sailing lingo but knew that meant they were getting ready to set sail at 9 am. They had been docked in Portland, Maine for over a week, stocking up on supplies for the trip ahead, trading, and visiting some of Conrad's old friends. During their stay, Noah thought a great deal about his father since he had spent so much time in Portland for work. He couldn't help but muse about the places he must have gone to regularly and the people he knew. A couple of times Noah mentioned his father's name, Martin Sullivan, to Conrad's friends but only one was familiar with him by reputation as a great lobsterman, though they never properly met. Somehow even that little bit of information made his father still seem alive somehow and he swelled with pride at the comment.

As intriguing as their time in Portland was, Noah was now getting a little restless to see his lovely Lily, but since Conrad had so generously agreed to take him along and shouldered a large portion of the cost, including the maintenance of the boat, he figured it was best not to complain.

Noah emerged from the cabin, onto the deck, and found Conrad fidgeting with the line that secured the boat to the dock. Conrad preferred to sleep under the stars when weather permitted and wake by the first light of day, so he had already been up for a couple of hours and was quite chipper. Noah could sense his mood because Conrad was whistling a lively tune and it seemed Conrad only whistled when he was feeling good—which was often. He looked up at Noah and gave him a toothy grin, "Hey, come over here will ya, and finish untying the boat so I can steer us out of here?"

Noah complied swiftly. It seemed so many of the tasks on the boat required two hands. He often wondered how Conrad usually managed it alone. No matter, within a few minutes they were pulling out of the dock and heading out to sea. Noah watched as the town of Portland shrank from view. It was an exciting town, one he felt connected to because of his father, but his eyes were set to the south on Boston. And then to a land of palm trees and coconuts. How odd it would be to go a whole year without winter, he thought. To escape the bitter cold of the harsh north would be a treat.

He stood at the head of the ship, enjoying the refreshing breeze that whipped through his shaggy blonde hair. The air was balmy and the sun was still somewhat low on the horizon, casting a brilliant golden hue that reflected on the water to the east. It would be a long day of sailing and with any hope, they would arrive early enough to go into town for a bite to eat and then get some rest so he could go meet Lily bright and early the next day. In the meantime, it appeared to be nothing but smooth sailing ahead.

CHAPTER TWO

It was late in the evening when *The Serenade* pulled into the Boston harbor. The sun had set an hour ago, though there were still traces of pink streaking across the sky casting a luminous reflection on the water. The sound of horns signaling the arrival of various boats filled the air. Conrad was steering them into the port, full of excitement as they gazed upon the city lights before them. He approached everything with the enthusiasm of a child, even the inconveniences. It was as if Conrad saw all occurrences as an opportunity for a new story to tell.

Noah, on the other hand, had his mind on one

thing—Lily. Sure, it hadn't been long since they parted, but already he missed her sweet smiling face and joyful spirit. No longer were there any misunderstandings between them. They had confessed their love and could make the most of the coming days together basking in the pleasure of each other's company and affection. But for now, both Noah and Conrad were hungry, so dinner was their first and foremost order of business.

Together they got the boat properly docked and secured in the marina then headed for the city streets to find an open public house for some cheap grub. Noah was astounded by the enormous size of the buildings in Boston. Aside from pictures in books, he had never seen a skyscraper or the vastness of a city that size. It overwhelmed him a bit as he thought about the special spot in the city park where he and Lily were to meet in the morning. He stated his hope that he wouldn't have trouble finding the meeting place, but then Conrad assured him that he could always ask any random "Chowdahead" for directions as Bostonians are nothing if not proud of their city. As they continued walking, they came upon an inviting tavern and agreed to stop in.

Noah and Conrad entered the low-lit establishment and immediately found a cozy table in the back corner. Inside people were scattered in clusters of 3 or 4, but many were talking to others in close proximity. The noisy chatter nearly drowned out the voice of the short, stocky server who came to take their order. He sported a faded tattoo on his right bicep of an anchor, and upon first inspection, he looked rather unapproachable. But despite appearances, he was in friendly spirits and seemed to make out their requests without difficulty even with the ruckus.

Noah, on the other hand, struggled to make out the man's thick Bostonian accent and mostly just nodded his head to not draw unnecessary attention to being from out of town. During his time working by the docks, he had run into a fair amount of people with that particular accent in the market, so there was still some familiarity with it, but not under such noisy experiences. Though they were known for being a bit surly, he couldn't help but admire the blunt, yet genuine manner in which they spoke. The server was no exception.

After the order was placed as best Noah could ascertain, he noticed one burly guy with flaming red hair was a little worse for the wear and began shouting belligerently at another intoxicated chap across the room wearing a brown faded ivy cap. From what Noah could decipher, it appeared the man in the cap had bumped into the red-haired man as he passed his table and didn't apologize for the disrespectful act. A moderately attractive woman in her thirties, who appeared to have done her share of hard living, came over to quiet him down, but Red was having none of it. He simply pushed her aside with his bear paw-like hands, nearly knocking her to the floor and the room got quiet as everyone stared at the common drunkard.

This caused the ivy-capped man to approach the table and he began cursing when Red gave him a sloppy blow to the jaw, causing the offending man to fall back against the chair behind him. He was more dazed than injured, but a fight was sure to break out any minute if this continued.

"Alright, that's enough Smitty," the bartender yelled, "I think it's time to call it a night."

Smitty didn't seem pleased by his demanding tone and turned to the bartender with a finger shaking in his face and slurred, "Don't staht with me, Lou. You see what happened to the last guy who tried to aggravate me."

Being larger and sober, Lou didn't seem humored by the threat and asserted himself further. "Smitty, if you say one more word, I'm throwing you outta here, ya undehstand?"

Smitty grunted under his breath and stumbled back into his seat, seemingly at a loss of mental capacity to respond with any wit. The woman who had tried to calm him put her arm around him, which he shrugged off. She seemed genuinely hurt by his callousness but smiled as if to hide it.

Shortly after the incident died down their food was brought out, which they ate quickly. Conrad appeared to be amused by the whole incident and said this was quite a common occurrence in the local pubs—that the Irish temper was mostly to blame but that most people got over these types of altercations quickly.

Once they finished their supper, Conrad and Noah began heading back to the boat for the night. Conrad had consumed a couple of drinks but didn't seem to have any trouble holding his liquor. For the most part, it just made him more jovial than he already was. Noah suspected he was no stranger to alcohol but seemed to minimize his intake for Noah's sake, since Noah knew little about such things, nor did he express much curiosity in them.

As they walked on toward the marina, Conrad spoke of his other visits to Boston in the past, including the time a guy bet him $5 that he couldn't get a pretty waitress to kiss him by the end of the night and how he won the bet but didn't take the money because the kiss was reward enough. Noah wrinkled his brow at the comments to which Conrad went on to explain that there are women with experience in kissing, among other things, that do a far better job than the shy ones who are only looking for husbands. Conrad roared at Noah's widening expression and added with a wink, "Kisses from those types of girls aren't worth the return! Give me a woman who knows what she's doing and expects nothing for it."

Noah was certain Conrad enjoyed getting a rise out of him. He then wondered what kind of girl would be so liberal in her affections to expect nothing in exchange, which fascinated him to consider, though he doubted such women actually existed. Everyone wants something, right?

Conrad then told another story about how he and buddy had been so down on their luck that they traded a tarnished pocket watch they found on the shore for a cheap fishing net only to find out later the watch was gold, but that they caught enough fish with the net to buy ten gold pocket watches. Conrad always had stories like that, and Noah was inclined to doubt half of his stories if his friends didn't seem to always go along with his crazy shenanigans. And he did seem to have an incredible effect on people, including Noah himself. Conrad was one of those guys everybody loved because he was always up for a good time and never cheated at cards, or so one of Conrad's friends in Portland had put it.

Once back at the boat, Noah prepared for a restful sleep. Conrad still seemed in a talkative mood, but Noah was spent. It was a long day, and he was eager to get up and meet with Lily. She was the anchor of his every thought. Even with all the excitement of Conrad's fantastical stories, he always kept his focus on his darling girl—she who had changed him so radically and caused him to have the courage to even face the sea and all these new foreign places.

Noah headed down to his bunker, but Conrad was still laughing over some other memory he shared. It sure seemed like the further they got from home that Conrad's tribal side came out. In Newland, he had seemed so steady and down to earth, a competent teacher, but it was as if the sea brought about some madness to his state of being and Noah wasn't sure what to make of it. On the one hand, it was thrilling to be along for the ride with one so full of life, but there was something that left him feeling a little uneasy about it too. He was too tired to figure it out that night, he thought, and with that, Noah drifted off sleep by the lull of the rocking ship bobbing gently in the harbor.

CHAPTER THREE

Noah was up with the sun and quickly got ready to go meet Lily. They were to meet at 8 am under a gazebo in the city park which was just a short walk from the marina. Even so, the thought of attempting to navigate the city streets alone was a bit overwhelming to Noah so he wanted to get an early start to avoid being late. Noah had yet another chance to demonstrate his growing independence. Sure, he and Lily had spent time all over Newland during her visit that summer, but now he was on her turf and wanted to make a good impression.

The air was crisp, and the streets were still quiet and

relatively empty, so Noah strolled lazily through the city, holding tight to the letter Lily gave him with the directions while keeping a watchful eye on the street names. He was just as astonished by the size of the city as he was the night before, perhaps more so being up close and surrounded by tall buildings in every direction. The sun was barely peeking through the narrow streets, blocked out by the intrusive towers. Suddenly he emerged from the tight cityscape and a vast green park lay before him, misty with the morning dew. His pulse quickened as he crossed the street and entered by way of the park entrance. It was just as Lily described and in an instant, he could make out part of the gazebo in the distance through the trees. It was early yet, so he did not expect Lily to be there, but Noah ran with anticipation just the same.

As he came into the clearing the gazebo was now in full view. Standing in the center was a figure in a flowing white gown with soft brown curls cascading over her shoulders. She caught sight of Noah and waved enthusiastically, and his heart leapt with joy at the sight. He couldn't believe Lily had arrived early as well, but he was thankful to not have to wait a moment longer to see her. He continued to run toward her so as not to limit their time together by even a few seconds.

Once he arrived at the base of the large gazebo, he flew up the steps to the platform where Lily was waiting expectantly, and they threw themselves into each other's arms for a warm, eager embrace. Noah could smell strawberries in her hair which flooded his senses with delicious delight. He didn't know how he could be taken from her yet again, but for now, they were together and had five glorious days to look forward to.

After their long-lasting embrace, they simultaneously pulled apart long enough for Noah to see Lily's fresh face, her round cheeks pink and shining from happiness. Her soft, smiling lips greeted his enthusiastically and suddenly Noah was at home in this strange city. "I can't believe you got here so early!" he said.

"Yes, well, I guess I couldn't sleep and so I decided to just rush over. Besides, I love the stillness of the morning…the city is rarely this peaceful. But I wasn't waiting long. I got here about five minutes before you."

Noah smiled. "Well, it sure was a welcomed sight, my dear, and how glad I am to finally get to see your new city. I can't wait to have you show me around to all the spots you've told me about."

Lily was delighted by Noah's enthusiasm. "Well, first things first. We need to head back home because mama and papa are eager to see you as well and want you to have breakfast with the family."

That sounded just fine with Noah. Lily lived in a hilly neighborhood, which was just a short walk. They hugged each other tightly one more time, Noah rocking Lily back and forth as he did, and then the two of them walked together hand in hand to the north side of the park. It was as though the birds were singing just for them as they went along.

They soon approached the regal brownstone where Lily and her family now lived. The door opened to reveal quite a stately home, adorned in rich wood trim and an enormous crystal chandelier overhead. It was a rental, but Noah couldn't help but marvel how elegant their abode in Boston was compared to the humble blue cottage in Maine—or Birchwood Cottage for that matter. Her father was quite well off at his new job, from the looks of it.

Lily's parents greeted Noah at the entrance with hugs and a warm welcome. Though their disposition was cheery, Noah couldn't help but take notice of the stress lines on Mr. Stephens's face which he didn't recall seeing before. Mrs. Stephens, on the other hand, was now getting quite large with child and glowed as though she were ten years younger. Her chestnut hair was pulled back into a loose bun and she was wearing an apron, which tightly clung to her round belly.

“I’m just finishing up the potatoes,” she said as she headed back into the kitchen, “Feel free to have a seat and relax. Breakfast will be ready in a bit!”

Noah took a seat on a warm, leather armchair and Lily’s Dad sat on a matching chair across from him. “So, son, how was your trip? Are you enjoying your time at sea?”

“Yes, sir!” Noah began with a hint of pride, “It’s been quite an experience so far. It took me a couple of days to get my sea legs but now I don’t get sick so much from the waves. We also had quite the grand time in Portland—picked up a lot of supplies and Conrad did some trading. I was amazed by the size of the city, but it was nothing like Boston though. I can’t imagine all the opportunities there must be to make a good living here.”

Mr. Stephens grinning countenance suddenly darkened. “Yes, well, big cities come with their own set of problems. It’s a very competitive world, Noah. If you hope one day to make your mark, just be sure that it doesn’t cost you your soul.”

Noah didn’t know what Lily’s father meant by that nor had he thought much about making his “mark”, but even this short time in Boston was beginning to open his eyes to the possibilities the world had to offer aside from being a fisherman. What would he want to do with his life if given the chance? There was so much more to the world than he imagined, so he'd have to think more on that later. In the meantime, Lily was listening to their conversation, smiling and not wanting to interrupt their friendly discourse. It gladdened her heart to see how quickly her parents, especially her father, had warmed up to Noah and made him feel accepted.

After a bit more catching up, Mrs. Stephens called out that breakfast was ready and the three of them quickly got up and filed into the dining room to take a seat at the large, cherrywood table that filled the length of the room. Mr. Stephens said grace, thanking God for Noah's safe arrival and for the beautiful day, then they feasted on scrambled eggs, crisp bacon, and fried potatoes.

CHAPTER FOUR

After breakfast, Lily packed a picnic lunch then she and Noah headed back out into the world for an afternoon of sightseeing and leisure. Lily wanted to give Noah the grand tour, not to mention it was an excuse for a little one on one time. Noah was taking in all of the sights as she described her first few months living in the new city and what a difficult adjustment it was for the family. She had lived in a big city in Virginia before moving to Maine, but besides missing Newland terribly, the culture was quite a bit different than both places and Lily wasn't sure she would ever fit in. She also explained how her father struggled to acclimate to his new high-pressure job and often expressed that perhaps his lowkey personality wasn't a good fit with the brusque Boston personalities he worked with. He would often come home discouraged and said he was struggling to keep up with their pace.

Noah felt this might have explained the way Mr. Stephens appeared. He really was no shark, but more of a gentle, southern soul. He (along with his friend Everett) had been partially responsible for saving Noah's life when he nearly drowned last year, so Noah had developed a deep affection for him since that day and was now touched with compassion over his struggle to adjust. From what he understood, the Stephens family moved to Maine in the first place to get a break after Lily's father had become overwhelmed with the stress of his occupation. Seeing firsthand what he was willing to give up financially for a life of ease was telling of just how much he must have needed the rest.

Next, they came upon Lily's school, which she was permitted to take a few days off from while Noah was in town—a rare exception made by her parents. The high brick walls were so imposing they kept any sound from escaping so that a person would hardly know that school was currently in session. Lily pointed to a window a couple of stories up to show where her homeroom was. She talked a bit about the classes she just started and said her art teacher had been impressed with her work so far, something she credited to Noah, as he was such a help to her in developing her skills.

Noah never took the credit but accepted her compliment with grace. The truth was, Lily was a blossoming painter in her own right and Noah encouraged her to develop her own unique style rather than insisting she imitate his.

"So, when was the last time you painted?" she asked.

"Not since I left Newland. I figured it wasn't practical to carry all my supplies on the small boat, but I miss it very much. I keep trying to take in all these mental images for reference later."

"Well, don't drop the brush for too long. The world needs your art, Noah."

He blushed at the kindness of her words. "I don't know about that, but I would love to build a little art studio for the two of us someday."

The very thought touched Lily's heart. "That sounds lovely. I look forward to it."

"I have just the room in Birchwood Cottage, you know."

"Oh?"

"Aunt Prissy's old sitting room. Now that she has moved out to go live in her husband's home, I think it would be the perfect spot. Her view is even better than mine, you can see more of the cove to the north. I have just the place to set your easel too, so you can look out at the horizon while the sun sets—and right in front of me so I can always watch you while I paint. That is where I get my inspiration."

It was Lily's turn to blush now. She had never seen herself as particularly beautiful, but when Noah stared at her as he did just then she felt like the most enchanting creature on the planet. In fact, once without her knowledge, he had painted her into a scene on the seashore, which was now her most prized possession for she was truly able to see herself through his eyes—a reminder of how precious she was to him. For now, though, the art studio seemed like a lifetime away.

Noah took Lily's hand and intertwined his fingers into hers, then raised the backside to kiss it gently before walking on. They decided to head back to the city park as it was an inviting day for a stroll. The weather was still fairly warm for late September and the ducks had not yet flown south. You could almost believe it was the middle of summer if not for the evidence of fall presenting itself through the turning of the leaves. Many of the trees still displayed a good amount of green, but their days were numbered.

Lily continued to lead Noah past the gazebo where they met earlier that morning and onward to an idyllic pond set in the middle of the city that was draped in weeping willows and scattered with swans as well as ducks and geese. A truly romantic setting for their afternoon together.

They crossed the bridge halfway over the pond then stopped to look out across the water that was framed by tall city buildings in the distance, towering over the treetops. Lily leaned over the railing and gleefully watched a pair of swans float lazily by. "Ooh aren't swans so breathtakingly exquisite?" She cooed.

Noah chuckled to himself. Having moved several times, Lily had seen quite a bit in her young life, yet she still got excited over things most people would consider an insignificant part of everyday life. But that was part of her charm. One thing was certain, life with her would never be dull.

They continued walking around the pond, talking about their dreams for the future, schooling, sailing, art, books, and everything in between. They found a perfect secluded grassy spot for their picnic under one of the willow trees by the pond. After laying out an old flannel blanket to sit on, they munched on crackers, an assortment of cheeses, and fresh-cut fruit. After having their fill, Noah sat against the trunk of the old willow while Lily laid on her back, her head resting comfortably in Noah's lap as he read a few verses from his favorite pocketbook of poems (one of the few personal items he brought with him on the trip).

As imperceptibly as Grief
The Summer lapsed away –
Too imperceptible at last
To seem like Perfidy –
A Quietness distilled
As Twilight long begun,
Or Nature spending with herself
Sequestered Afternoon –
The Dusk drew earlier in –
The Morning foreign shone –
A courteous, yet harrowing Grace,
As Guest, that would be gone –
And thus, without a Wing
Or service of a Keel
Our Summer made her light escape
Into the Beautiful.

After he finished the last stanza, Lily sighed contentedly, "I can't imagine a more perfect day. I wish it didn't have to end."

"Never fear, my lady, I'll be back tomorrow to do it all

again!"

Lily smiled and looked up at the fluffy clouds floating overhead. She couldn't make out their shapes, due to the branches, but it was a peaceful sight. She knew there weren't many days like this left. "You know, the only thing that could make this day better would be sitting like this on the beach back home in Newland."

Noah closed his eyes for a moment to picture it. He had only been gone a short while, but it felt a million miles away. "That would be pleasant too, but I could be happy anywhere with you," he replied in earnest.

Lily sighed once more, only this time wistfully. "Oh Noah, how are we going to make it through the next nine months after a day like today?"

"Don't worry, my dear, you'll be so busy with your studies you won't have time to miss me, and then I'll be back before you know it. There to wreak more havoc on your perfect life in Boston."

"Oh, don't tease so Noah, I am terribly distressed at the thought." Lily frowned prettily.

"That's funny, I've always thought you quite independent and determined. What has happened to my spirited girl?" He asked, further teasing despite her protest.

Lily then sat up and gazed dreamily into his cool blue

eyes, "What can I say, Noah? I've been captured and tamed."

Noah felt the heat emanating from Lily's sultry gaze and pulled her in for a kiss that intensified with every passing second. Her hands were in his hair now, pulling him deeper into her inviting lips. One thing Lily had not lost was her passion. Noah gently pulled away from the embrace to catch his breath. His mind raced back to what Conrad said about girls looking for a husband and soundly concluded this notion of bad kissing did not apply to Lily. "Easy does it there," he said, placing his hand between them to cool down.

Lily played coy. "What?"

"You know very well what. Don't work your feminine charms on me, missy. If you're trying to get me to stay, it's working."

Lily gave a look of angelic innocence. "I don't know what you're talking about," she breathed.

Noah raised an eyebrow and gave a look that said he wasn't buying it. "You know, I would if you really wanted me to." He was serious now. He'd be lying if he didn't say that being there with Lily now didn't make him second guess the trip.

Lily now felt a pang of guilt for abusing her charms. "Well, tempting as it is, I'm not going to trick you into staying, but it's nice to know I could if I wanted to." Lily grinned then looked down to avert Noah's gaze, "In all seriousness though, I know you need to do this for yourself Noah, and for us. Not because I want us to be apart, but after everything you've been through it's time you did something for yourself while you still can. I never want you to have regrets. I know fulfilling your dreams will make you a better man—and perhaps a husband someday."

Noah wasn't sure how he felt about what she said but he loved her for it. Perhaps she was right. Maybe this was something he needed to do. It was now or never, and aside from seeing some of the world, his love for sailing was growing. Maybe one day he would be confident enough in his skills that he and Lily could go on a sailing adventure of their own. Now there was a glorious thought!

They basked in the afternoon sun a while longer before agreeing it was time to pack up their belongings, then they headed back to Lily's house to spend the rest of the day with the family. Noah finally left to head back to the boat just as the sun was beginning to set but promised to meet Lily the following day under the gazebo, same time as before. Tomorrow she wanted to show off more of the waterfront and perhaps take him to the town square, which bustled with all kinds of shops and historical sites. Noah couldn't wait to spend another fun-filled day with his sweetheart. He thought of nothing else as he walked back to the marina, not even noticing Conrad screaming his name and waving his arms frantically.

CHAPTER FIVE

Noah had closed the distance considerably by the time he recognized Conrad's voice. He looked up from his reverie, his eyes searching for the direction of his name. Once he spotted Conrad's location he sprinted to where he stood, his mind racing at the possibilities for his desperate cries.

"We have to leave Noah, tonight."

Noah couldn't comprehend the words that were coming from Conrad's lips. "What do you mean, tonight? We're supposed to be here for the week!" It was only then that Noah noticed Conrad wasn't alone. Standing next to him was the attractive, but tough-looking woman he had seen at the bar the night before. She now had a red mark blazing across her pale cheek.

The woman interjected, "I was telling Conrad, Smitty is looking for him. You don't know what he's capable of. He will surely kill him if he finds him. He went out to gather some of his pals but he'll back soon."

Conrad may have been a man of experience, but he was not the fighting type. He did his best to always avoid trouble when possible and today was not a good day to die.

"I don't understand, why would that man Smitty want to kill Conrad?" Noah's eyes darted from the woman and then back to Conrad, seeking answers to this unexpected turn of events.

"I will let you tell him, Conrad. For now, I must go before Smitty realizes I'm gone. Hurry, leave while you still have the chance! Smitty's contacts are everywhere." And with that, she gave one last look at Conrad before fleeing through the streets and disappearing around a corner.

"I don't get it, Conrad, what is going on?"

"Let's get back to the boat and I'll fill you in. All I can tell you right now is that we can't stay."

As the seriousness of the situation sunk in, Noah was filled with dread at having to leave Lily. He had to get to the bottom of this. If Conrad was in trouble, he needed to hear him out and see if there was any chance of getting out of this predicament. Once they reached the boat, Conrad climbed aboard cautiously to make sure no one was waiting for him above deck or below. After searching the cabins, he called Noah to join him below.

Conrad was frantic but jumped into his story for he felt he didn't have a moment to lose. "Look Noah, I need you to hear me out. I honestly didn't know." Noah wasn't sure how to react so he simply nodded for him to continue. "After you went to bed last night I was still feeling a bit restless. I usually am on the first night in a new port. Anyway, I went back to the pub and when I got there that Smitty fellow had left and I ended up talking to Geraldine, that's the lady you just met. Anyway, she was still crying over what happened earlier and I was trying to cheer her up. We had a few drinks and stayed up late...*talking*. Anyway, we planned to meet up this afternoon and after some time she took me back to her place for a bit. We were only there a short while when Smitty came home unexpectedly. I didn't realize they were married! Anyway, once she heard him coming up the walk she had me slip out the back door, but he came inside before I could leave and he flew into a fit of rage and tried to catch me. I may not be strong, but I am fast. I ran out the back but not before he caught sight of me. He was yelling and cursing something terrible and the last thing I heard was Geraldine scream."

There was a pause but Noah said nothing, so Conrad continued. "Well, I went back into town and Geraldine found me near the docks when she explained that Smitty was out looking for me. Apparently, he is known for being a surly sort who has killed men for less. He once burned a man alive in his sailboat while he slept for cheating him in cards. It sounds like we don't have much time to lose, so we have to shove off now."

Noah took everything in and was still processing the thought of leaving so suddenly. "But Lily…"

"I'm sorry Noah, you're gonna have to write her and let her know what happened and hope she'll understand."

"But I can't just leave her, she'll be waiting for me in the morning. What will she think if I don't show? She'll think I'm dead or something." Noah was getting more frantic with each passing minute. He would not put her through the worry.

"Well, you can stay here if you need to, but I'm heading out tonight."

Noah thought for a moment before speaking, weighing his options. "Listen, can't we please just stay for the night? I am supposed to meet Lily first thing in the morning. Let me go to her and explain the situation and then you can leave immediately afterward."

Conrad considered Noah's idea but hesitated, "I don't know…"

"*Please.* Smitty can't possibly know who you are or where your boat is docked. I'm sure you can buy enough time and lay low until morning. I'll be back before 9 am."

Conrad relented, "I'll tell you what I can do. I will dock the boat down the coast a bit, that should buy us some time, but you'll have to be back here by 9 am or I'm leaving—with or without you. Deal?"

Noah dropped his face into his hands and thanked Conrad for giving him the opportunity to work things out. His heart was grieved by the prospect of his time in Boston being cut short, but he was grateful he wouldn't have to leave without saying goodbye to Lily first. He had some decisions ahead of him and for the rest of the night he tossed and turned as he weighed his options, which weren't looking too bright from any angle.

Noah was up at dawn and wanted to head out quickly to work

his way toward the gazebo where he and Lily were to meet again. Conrad had anchored the ship for the night about two miles south and then dropped him off at a different marina in the morning. It was only a slight distance from the channel they were docked before, but Noah was concerned once again about finding the spot since he would be heading from a different direction. Conrad gave him some general directions to help him get back on track, which was helpful, but didn't eliminate his anxiety altogether. To make matters worse, the weather had turned overnight and along with a cold front came rain. It was only coming down lightly now, and in Noah's haste, he forgot to grab his poncho.

For the first few blocks Noah was so lost in thought he barely noticed the light droplets gradually saturating his hair and clothes. He didn't know how he was going to break the news to Lily. She was sure to be as greatly disappointed as he was. What plans they had for the day! The rainfall increased as he went and soon he could no longer ignore it. At one point he considered whether or not he should head back to the boat for his poncho, but he had gone too far and did not want to lose more time. Instead, he decided to pick up the pace by running.

Soon small puddles began forming in the crevices of the city streets. It was becoming increasingly difficult to make out anything more than a block ahead of him. Thankfully, the directions Conrad gave were simple. His biggest concern was missing his turn, so he watched each street name carefully as he passed. As the day before, there were fewer people out that early, which helped not to slow him down, but the rain was doing a good job on its own.

At one point, Noah was sure he was lost. The city was congested, and the roads crisscrossed so much he wondered if he had passed the street he was to turn on or if he veered off the street he was on without his knowledge. He called out to a heavy-set man outside a hotel pushing a laundry cart and asked if he could tell him where to find the street. The man grunted and simply pointed, apparently in no mood for chit chat, but Noah found out all he needed to know. He had not yet come upon it, so he ran on, his anxiety increasing with each passing minute. He prayed Lily would be early again for they had no time to spare.

As Noah neared the park, he began to recognize his surroundings and breathed a sigh of relief. He stepped onto the green from the south end this time but was forced to slow his running to a trot, as the grassy park had become soggy with mud. Despite his caution, Noah still managed to slip on the slick grass and fell swiftly on his side. His pants and shirt were smeared with mud, the bulk of which began running off immediately as the rain continued to pelt him. He picked himself back up and continued on at a rapid pace.

As he approached the gazebo his heart caught in his throat. There was Lily, standing front and center once again, holding a bag and umbrella at her side and smiling brightly as if the sun were shining and she wasn't waiting in a rainstorm for her love to be dragged away from her. However, once she caught sight of Noah her smile quickly faded. Something seemed wrong.

Noah didn't even bother with the steps this time. He heaved himself up onto the gazebo platform and stood before Lily, trying to catch his breath. Lily set her belongings carefully on the ground and reached out to touch his soaked arms.

"What in the world is going on, Noah? Didn't you even think to bring an umbrella or something, you poor dear?" She chided him lightly, a look of genuine concern on her face.

Noah didn't waste another second. "Lily my dear, listen, I don't have much time, but I have some bad news…"

"What do you mean? What's going on, Noah?" She interrupted as the urgency in Noah's voice began to rise.

"It's Conrad. He's gotten himself in a bit of trouble and he means to head out of Boston this very morning. If I'm not back by 9 am he is leaving without me."

Lily's brow creased. "What kind of trouble? Does it

involve you?"

"No, it has nothing to do with me, but he could be in terrible danger. He wanted to leave last night but I begged him to wait until morning. Oh Lily, I just couldn't leave like that!"

The tears were coming hot and fast down her cheeks now. "I don't understand Noah, why do you have to leave so suddenly? Isn't there anything that can be done?"

"I'm afraid not." How Noah wished he could tell her otherwise. "There's a guy after him. He's got a reputation. He's killed men. He might try to kill Conrad and he knows it won't be long before he's found. I was lucky to even talk him into staying for the night."

Lily was still so confused as she processed the crushing blow of knowing the time she planned with Noah was coming to a sudden end. Noah didn't wish to hold her in suspense and quickly explained the whole salacious affair between Conrad, Geraldine, and Smitty.

Lily's eyes narrowed as the details came to light. "So, you're telling me he just picked up some man's wife from the tavern? Well, what did he expect?"

"It wasn't like that Lily, Conrad didn't know. He swore he had no idea."

"Well, it sounds to me like his first mistake was getting involved with a woman he didn't really know."

Even though Noah had thought the same thing he was feeling a little defensive of Conrad now. “I told you, he was trying to comfort her. If you had seen the way this Smitty guy treated her the night before you would understand too. He practically threw her on the ground.”

Lily wasn’t sure she was buying it, but Conrad had been good to Noah and she trusted Noah completely and decided to give him the benefit of the doubt by not commenting further. “So, what now?”

“We have a few minutes together before I have to head back or…”

“Or what?”

Noah clasped his hands together in a praying position as he carefully considered his next suggestion. “I could stay. I know yesterday we said I should go, but that’s before all this happened. Just say the word and I’ll go back and get my belongings and stay in Boston with you.”

Lily was silent for a moment as she considered his proposal. More than anything she wanted to be with Noah, but aside from losing a few days together, she concluded nothing had changed. She still wanted him to fulfill his dreams and she still needed to concentrate on her schooling. Asking him to move to Boston when there were no guarantees was selfish. “No, you have to go,” she finally replied.

Noah was astonished by her response, perhaps even a little hurt. "Why?"

"You know why." She said softly, "We've already talked about it. Listen Noah, we had our beautiful day together. A day full of memories to last a lifetime. Don't give up your plans for this year because we weren't able to have a few more. I mean, we had two full months—how greedy can we get? Besides, when you get back we'll have so many more like it, even better."

Tears were streaming down Lily's face again and now even Noah began to cry, "But I don't know if I can. Not this way." Noah held Lily's cold, white hands in his and gazed into her sad, loving eyes.

"Be strong Noah. I can be strong if you are strong."

And that was all he needed. Lily had always been the strong one between them, but it was his turn to be strong and he managed to choke out, "Okay. I'll go. But it won't be easy."

Lily somehow forced a smile through the tears, "I know you can do it, Noah. You've never let me down before."

Noah now put his hands on Lily's face, cupping it gently. His eyes searched her features so that he might not forget a detail while he was gone. "I will do my best to never disappoint you, Lily. I owe everything to you." He then kissed her lips and her damp, tear-stained cheeks and back to her lips again. Such sweet, tender kisses might sustain him, Noah thought as he held Lily close in a tight embrace. They were both wet now from tears and the cold rain that the wind continuously blew into the gazebo. They exchanged a few more words of comfort before they both knew it was time for Noah to depart.

"Oh my goodness, I almost forgot!" Lily exclaimed. "I had an early birthday present for you." She handed him the bag she had set on the platform.

Noah smiled at the gesture and opened the bag, eager to know what thoughtful thing Lily had done this time. She didn't disappoint. Inside was a leather-bound sketchbook and a group of five drawing pencils tied together with a red piece of yarn.

"I figured since you couldn't paint on your trip, you might still do some sketching. Ya know, so you can remember all the places you've been and still keep up your skills."

Noah wanted to hug them to his chest, but then remembered he was still quite wet. Instead, he placed them carefully back in the bag and embraced his darling Lily one final time before kissing her goodbye. A kiss he made sure she would not soon forget.

CHAPTER SIX

The rain began to let up as Noah drew nearer to the marina. He had stuck the bag with the gift Lily gave him under his shirt so that it would stay dry. He was quick to get through the city streets and to the agreed upon location where Conrad said he would pick him up. With so many boats in the harbor, it was a little confusing to find the right dock but as he was searching the rows he recognized the red-haired man from the pub, Smitty, talking to two other equally beefy men.

To avoid being seen, Noah ducked behind a nearby boat and worked his way closer to where the men stood to get a closer listen.

"I know he's in here somewhere, I can feel it," Smitty said to his two friends. "Pauly told me he was certain the guy we're looking for sailed into the hahbor this morning, dropped off some kid, then headed back out to sea. Something tells me he'll be back. He said the name on the boat was *The Serenade,* so keep a lookout."

The other men stood silently with their arms crossed looking around the marina for a sign of the boat. Noah knew he had no time to lose. He had to find Conrad and warn him so they could leave as soon as possible. Continuing to lay low and weaving in between the boats, Noah was concerned that if he was spotted that the thugs might begin to get curious and start asking questions. Still, if he was seen sneaking around the marina that would look awfully suspicious too.

Soon Noah no longer heard the men's voices and hoped they had gone away, but just to be safe he continued keeping his head down. Suddenly he spotted *The Serenade,* sails up and flapping proudly against the blustery wind. Conrad was on deck and caught sight of Noah and called out, "Hey there kid, time's up, let's get going!" Noah tried to signal back to keep his voice down, but Conrad was oblivious to the gesture and continued to yell. "Hey what are you doing, stop fooling around, it's time to shove off!"

Suddenly the voice of a man called out from the other side of the marina, "There he is, that's the fella, go get em' boys!"

Noah knew his time was up and gave up his hiding spot, running toward the sailboat in a full sprint. Conrad's eyes were wide as he watched the three burly men barreling toward him. Noah jumped into the boat quickly and wasted no time untying the knots to set themselves free. In response, Conrad quickly jumped to the Captain's wheel and began slowly backing the ship out, the wind giving them all the inertia needed, but not before Smitty and his men arrived. One jumped from the dock, grabbed onto the edge of the sailboat, and worked to pull himself up into it, but Conrad steered him into the dock, which caused him to scream in pain and drop his grip. The madman fell into the water, causing a huge splash and as he leveled unintelligible curses at them.

Smitty was still standing on the dock's edge and pulled out a pistol and began shooting erratically in their direction. Conrad ducked behind the steering wheel and Noah jumped straight down into the cabin, missing the steps altogether. He heard the gun go off again but heard no screams of pain so he assumed Smitty missed again. The boat was moving faster now which meant they must have pulled out and were heading into the harbor.

Noah heard no further gunshots, so he felt it was probably safe to sneak back up onto the deck and check on Conrad. When he emerged, he saw they were indeed heading out toward the open ocean and Conrad was feeling safe enough to stand tall at the helm. The men left standing on the docks were getting smaller by the second, but Noah could still see the rage as they shook their fists at them. It was a close call, but somehow, they made it out unscathed.

Noah was still a bit shaken up when he heard Conrad laughing hysterically. He was shocked to find him behaving so. "How can you laugh at a time like this? We were nearly killed!"

"The keyword is 'nearly'. We can laugh now. Did you see the look on Smitty's face? And that guy when he fell into the water? Boy, were they mad!"

"I'll say," Noah said, still struggling to find the humor in it, "But I don't think you'll be wanting to go back to Boston any time soon. Any chance they might try to follow us?"

"Nah," Conrad was quite at ease now, "The girl isn't worth the hassle. Now maybe for a buxom blonde or a young high-class lady, but girls like Geraldine are a dime a dozen to guys like Smitty. They'll either work things out or he'll find another one like her."

Noah couldn't believe his ears. How could someone be

so callous about their wife? "If she didn't mean anything to him, why did he even bother to chase you down at all?"

"This was all about respect. He couldn't have his girl or his friends thinking he was a pushover or that he would let some out of towner take his woman without a fight. Truth is, Geraldine is quite sweet and probably would have made him a good wife if he treated her half decent. But I meant what I told you, I really didn't know they were married. Guys like Smitty aren't usually the marrying kind."

Noah believed him but still wondered why he bothered spending time with Geraldine at all when he knew they were leaving in a few days. *What kind of relationship could come out of being with someone for such a short time?* He pondered. No matter, they were heading out for the open sea once again and Noah was battling mixed feelings between leaving Lily so suddenly and his excitement for the adventure that lay ahead.

"So how did she take it?" Conrad asked after a time when things settled down.

"About as well as you'd expect. She was disappointed, of course, but she wanted me to continue on my trip."

"Oh, was there ever any question?" Conrad kept a close watch on Noah's reply.

"Well, honestly I did consider staying but she

reminded me of why I was going in the first place and that it won't be long before we'll be together again…for good."

Deep down Conrad was relieved. He may have been willing to make good on his threat about leaving if Noah was late, but deep down he enjoyed the young man's company and was looking forward to teaching him more about sailing and the sea. "Well, it sounds like you really do have a rare catch there. Better hold onto that one."

Noah nodded, but he didn't need Conrad to tell him that. If there was one thing he was absolutely certain of in this life, it was that Lily Stephens was the best thing that ever happened to him. He then remembered the present tucked into his shirt, so he pulled it out to take a closer look at it. Thankfully it had only suffered minor water damage from the rain but otherwise was in tip-top shape. Once they got going Noah pulled out one of the pencils and began to sketch a memory of a face he could never forget.

CHAPTER SEVEN

Lily watched with tears glistening in her eyes as the boy she loved walked away and out of sight. It was only then that she felt she could finally set her emotions free. She fell to her knees, placing her head in her hands, sobbing full stop. Letting him go was the hardest thing she had ever done. In her heart she wanted him to stay with her, to begin living out their days together at once, but she knew it would be a selfish request.

So long she had endured their separation, but it was harder the deeper she fell in love with him. Even more now than when she saw him just a month ago in Newland. He was taking up permanent residency in her heart and though she didn't doubt his love for her one bit, her secret insecurity was that others would also see in him the special qualities she recognized and want him for themselves. But that was not her pressing heartache. It was knowing they wouldn't be able to communicate at all between now and when he reached Florida. She didn't have the address she could write to him but would have to remain patient, even to hear that he arrived safely.

After wiping the tears from her eyes, Lily collected herself, grabbed her umbrella, and began heading for home. As she walked, she thought of their previous day together and the various locations they walked through, holding hands and laughing as carefree as an ocean breeze. The rain began to dissipate as she approached the brownstone-lined street she lived on. The fashionable brick homes were a beautiful sight among the misty rain-swept streets. She approached her doorstep and hesitated before walking in. How sad it was to come home alone, without Noah by her side. She dreaded having to explain the situation to her parents.

She walked through the front door and into the foyer when she heard her parents speaking in low, hushed tones. It sounded serious but their conversation ceased when they noticed Lily had approached.

"Hey honey, we didn't expect to see you back so soon.

Did you get rained out?" her mother said. Then noticing she was alone added, "Where is Noah? Is he still outside?"

"No mama." Lily swallowed hard. "Noah had to leave today. Something came up with Conrad and he couldn't stay." She didn't feel like going further into detail.

"Oh sweetie, that's terrible," her father chimed in. "What happened?"

"I can't really say. He had to leave quickly. It's alright though, we know we'll see each other again soon enough." She wasn't able to hide her disappointment completely, but her parents seemed distracted enough that they didn't take notice. Lily went up the stairs to her room on the second floor to mourn in private. She laid down on her bed, not bothering to change out of her damp clothes, and drifted off into a restless sleep.

A short time later a peel of thunder startled her awake and Lily sat up to see a storm was raging outside her window. It was not uncommon this time of year, but the rain contributed to her already morose state of mind. She got up to take a closer look outside the window when a flash of lightning blinded her followed by another earth-shattering crash of thunder. The storm was right on top of them.

Feeling unsettled, she went back downstairs into the sitting room to find her mother pacing frantically. "What's going on, Mama?" She asked.

Her mother jumped at the sound of her voice but then softened at the sight of Lily. "Nothing dear, just pray for your papa. He's going through a rough time at work. He headed out a bit ago." She instinctively caressed her belly as if soothing the baby inside of her womb.

Lily knew her father had not been too happy since they moved to Boston, but she was more concerned now. Something definitely seemed wrong. She said a quick prayer then asked her mother if she could help with any chores. She hoped doing some work around the house might be a good distraction for her. Lily's mother seemed to appreciate the offer and pointed her in the direction of the kitchen.

"Actually, would you mind washing the dishes from last night? I meant to get to it first thing this morning, but some things came up. I sure would appreciate that honey."

Lily did as her mother requested without hesitation. She usually did the dishes anyway, but when she still had plans with Noah her mother offered to give her a break from doing them for a few days. She guessed there was no longer a need, so it was her chore anyway. Just as she assumed she would return to school the next day.

After the dishes were cleaned Lily noticed her mother was no longer in the sitting room. She assumed she must have gone to lie down and rest a bit, so Lily went back upstairs to her bedroom, but she wasn't entirely sure she didn't hear the faint sounds of sobbing as she passed her parent's room. Apparently, this wasn't shaping up to be a good day for anyone in the Stephens family.

Lily decided to pull out her journal and began writing. This was one of Lily's common pastimes, but rather than detailing her day, she found journaling to be an excellent source of emotional release. She often shared her secret thoughts and worked through them so they wouldn't stay locked inside her brain, swirling like a bubbling pot of stew. Luckily, her parents respected her space so she never feared they would read it. Not that what she said was especially concerning, but it would embarrass her to be so vulnerable with her most tender feelings. Not to mention, a great deal of her writing was nothing more than imperceptible ramblings. Her final assessment of any given situation usually emerged at a later time after she sorted through all the nonsense.

Today her penmanship suffered. She scratched out her feelings quickly, mostly sentiments of self-pity, then laid her head down for another good cry. This was doing her no good, so she decided to paint instead. She went over to her closet to pull out her easel when she came upon a painting she did earlier that year of a boy on a sailboat. She had completed this piece before Noah had expressed interest in sailing and in some way it almost seemed prophetic. She wondered where he was now and how he had fared through the storm.

Lily placed the painting back against the closet wall and proceeded to gather her supplies for an afternoon of painting. It somehow made her feel closer to Noah just then. They had spent a great deal of time painting together and found much joy in their friendship through it. He was a brilliant artist, sure to have a successful career someday. Lily was inspired by his use of color and light but couldn't quite master the technique. Still, her own artistic abilities had come a long way. Though she saw herself as nothing more than a hobbyist, Noah praised her work generously, and without any hint of condescension. He truly did feel she saw the world through a unique lens and would often remind her that the most commercially successful artists were not always the most technically skilled—it's about creating something that speaks to the heart of man.

Lily didn't know if her work spoke to anyone's heart, aside from Noah's, but she did appreciate his encouragement. Even now she found some pleasure in reflecting on his words and wondered at how he would go the rest of his trip without painting. *Hopefully the sketchbook I gave him will suffice*, she thought to herself.

Lily spent the rest of the afternoon working on a new piece inspired by their afternoon by the pond. She enjoyed implementing the use of long strokes for the limp branches of the willow tree and included a pair of swan mates beneath it. Aside from breaking for lunch, she was so consumed with her work that she didn't notice the hours passing. Her mother seemed pensive throughout the day and Lily didn't want to trouble her by asking too many questions so she did her best to stay out of the way.

It wasn't until the sun began to set, darkening the corners of her bedroom, that Lily noticed how late it was getting. It was already 8 pm but she had not heard her mother call up to her for dinner. She emerged from the room and into the hallway that led down the stairs, which was even more dimly lit. All was still and Lily realized she had not heard her father come in from work. She trotted down the steps to see what was going on.

Lily's mother was sitting in her father's armchair, looking at the clock and then looking at the door. She was clearly worried which made Lily nervous as well. "Where's papa?" Lily asked without hesitation.

"I don't know, it's really not like him to be late."

Dinner was warming on the stove and the table was set but her father had not come home at his usual time of 6 pm. Lily was about to suggest they go look for him when her father stumbled through the door. He was clumsy and disheveled, his tie hanging loose around his neck and his hair a rumpled mess. He was drunk.

"What is the meaning of this, Peter?" Her mother demanded.

"It's all over Marla, our time in Boston has come to an end." He slurred before sliding down the door and passing out on the floor.

CHAPTER EIGHT

Noah wasn't sketching for long when the boat started rocking back and forth intensely, making it impossible for him to continue on. He climbed out of the cabin and saw the rain had picked back up. Conrad was wearing his yellow slicker and struggling to pull down a sail when he noticed Noah watching him.

"Hey, come over here and help me why don't ya?" Conrad asked through gritted teeth. "There is a storm rolling in and we need to get these sails down."

Noah immediately jumped to assist Conrad by taking down the jib while Conrad finished taking down the mainsail.

Once both sails were properly folded down, Conrad returned to the helm to keep the boat steered toward the oncoming waves.

"I think we're just going to lie ahull," Conrad shouted through the rain. "I don't think the storm surge should be too great, hopefully we can just wait it out. Go get suited up and then get back on deck and help me keep watch."

Noah moved swiftly back down the stairs and put on his poncho, hat, and boots. This was the first storm he ever sailed through and he was both riveted and anxious at the thought. He returned quickly to where Conrad was standing and found it was becoming increasingly difficult to keep his balance. He decided to sit and wait for further direction. Conrad was calm and composed. For all his boyish antics, he took his position as Captain of *The Serenade* seriously. "Respect the sea" was his mantra and he had done well to teach Noah to do the same in their many lessons.

Flashes of lightning now graced the southern skyline and thunder roared in the distance. For the moment they were only battling 3-foot waves, but they were steadily increasing. Noah clung to his seat, closing his eyes and bracing for the incoming torrent of wind and rain.

It only took about ten minutes for the front end of the storm to reach them. Conrad held tight to the wheel, guiding them masterfully through the rushing waves. Higher and higher the boat climbed the mountainous swells and dipped low as each one passed. Noah wasn't sure if he was thrilled or terrified by the experience but seeing the cool look on Conrad's face gave him confidence that all would be well. This was Conrad at his very best.

It wasn't long before the worst was behind them. Conrad estimated the highest waves were somewhere around 6-feet high. Not incredibly dangerous, but it gave them a good ride for sure. It was only drizzling now and the sun was peeking through the clouds ahead. Boston was only a memory and now they were headed toward their destination with minimal stops along the way. Along with the rain came a fresh beginning and all new possibilities but the love of the sea was already deep in Noah's soul.

Lily was shocked and frightened at her father's behavior. Never in her seventeen years had she seen him in such a state. Aside from the occasional beer, she had never known her father to be intoxicated. Now he was laying passed out drunk on the floor before she and her mother.

Lily's mother acted quickly to tend to her husband. "Peter, wake up. Peter, can you hear me?" She pressed as she tried to flip him over onto his back. Lily was ready to take action to help her mother in any way she could but didn't say a word.

At last, her father began to groan and mumbled something about being "so sorry."

"Lily, go get me a cloth and some cold water." Her mother demanded.

Lily swiftly returned with the items and her mother began patting her father's forehead with a cold compress. His head tossed back and forth as he continued his unintelligible mumbling. Lily was scared, but her mother remained calm. "Is he going to be alright?" she asked, a tremble in her voice.

"Yes dear, I'm sorry you had to see your father like this, but he'll be fine by morning. Let's see if we can get him onto the sofa." The two ladies mustered up the strength to help Mr. Stephens to his feet until he stumbled a few feet and then crashed onto the sofa without much effort. Lily's mom grabbed the afghan that was draped over its backside and covered her husband tenderly. "It looks like he'll be okay, he just needs to sleep it off. Why don't you go up to bed too, honey?"

Lily wanted to stay in case her father needed more help, but she didn't want to disobey her mother and frustrate her further. She began her slow ascent up the stairs, silently praying for her father and wondering what he meant about their time in Boston being at an end. *How I wish Noah were here now.* She thought to herself, but it was too late. Noah was long gone and this was something she would have to face alone.

Lily didn't fall asleep immediately. She was deeply troubled, and her usual perky spirit dampened by the recent events. She woke up early the next morning, and though still feeling quite groggy, she raced down the stairs to see how her father was doing.

The sofa was empty, the afghan still strewn across the cushions, and she could hear her parent's voices coming from the dining room. She entered the doorway and saw her father sitting in his usual seat, holding a mug in one hand and his head in the other. He was definitely doing better than the night before, but not fully recovered. Her mother sat beside him with her hand on the arm that was holding the coffee.

"How is papa?" She asked anxiously. Her mother motioned for her to keep her voice down.

"He's doing okay this morning, but we must not speak

too loud." A groan escaped her father's lips just then. "Lily, your father and I want to talk to you when you get home from school today."

"School? Do I really have to go at a time like this?"

"I think it's best for today. Your father and I have some things to discuss and you need to stay focused on your studies."

Lily knew her mother was right but the idea of going to school after everything that took place the previous day was overwhelming. How was she going to focus on her studies knowing some major development may be awaiting her at home? Still, she did as her mother requested, went back upstairs to get ready for the day, then headed out the door—but not before giving her father a gentle kiss on the cheek. She may not understand everything that was going on with him, but he was her papa and had always been there for her, so now it was her turn to support him in whatever way she could.

CHAPTER NINE

It was half-past three when Lily arrived home that afternoon. She swiftly ran back to the brownstone townhouse after school let out, not lingering to join the chatter of her schoolmates as she often did. She did her best to concentrate on her classes throughout the day but struggled immensely, her father's words replaying over in her mind. Her head swirled with questions as to what could be going on with her father and what it meant for the future of their family.

When she walked in the door she was surprised to find things had changed considerably from when she left that morning. Furniture was covered in sheets and wooden crates scattered throughout the sitting room, half full with their belongings. Her parents were nowhere to be seen when suddenly her mother emerged from her father's study, wearing an apron and a scarf on her head.

"What's going on, mama?" Lily asked at once.

"I'm so glad you're home dear, come quickly. Your father is in his study packing up his things but he's doing much better. Why don't we go in there so we can all talk?"

Lily followed her mother into the dimly lit room, lined with bookshelves and a writing desk in the center. Her father was sitting at the desk and the shelves were now bare, the books and knick-knacks presumably packed away in the boxes stacked against the wall.

"Papa, is everything okay? Mama said you wanted to speak to me now. Please tell me what's going on." Lily's eyes begun to sting with tears.

Her father reached out his arms to pull her nearer. "Come here honey, there is nothing to be upset about. I'm sorry about last night." Lily was now hugging her father around the neck, hoping that all he said was true. She needed her father's reassurance now more than ever. He loosened his grip and looked at her concerned face. "Honestly everything's going to be okay. Look, there have been some difficulties at the office these past few months, so your mother and I discussed it and have decided it's time to go. We're going back to Newland—back to the blue cottage. That will be our forever home. See, it's not so bad, is it? You love Newland. So be a good girl and help your mother and I pack up."

Lily was stunned. What had caused everything to change so suddenly? It was so unlike her mother to encourage such a spontaneous decision. She had resisted when they left Virginia the previous year and was the reason her father felt compelled to take the job in Boston. "What kind of difficulties, papa? Are you in trouble?" She asked.

Lily's father was dismissive, "Now don't you go worrying your pretty little head about such things. Everything is alright. You have nothing to be concerned about. But we do have to leave quickly, so be a good girl and go help your mama. She's in no condition to pack this house up by herself."

Mrs. Stephens forced a smile to hide the look of worry on her brow. Lily wanted to believe everything was fine, but something felt strange in her gut. Still, she would have to admit that the idea of moving back to Newland didn't upset her terribly. In fact, there was no place on earth she would rather live. Now she and Noah could be together again— *Oh wait, Noah is on his way to Florida. What will he think when he finds out we're back in Newland?* Lily knew it would probably be another month before he arrived in Florida, maybe longer if

Conrad decided to linger at one of the ports. But she would have to worry about that later, for now, she asked her mother how she might help.

The two of them finished packing up the living room, Lily helping with the heavy lifting as much as possible, and then her mother asked her to go upstairs and start packing up her room. "Pack a travel bag too, dear. Be sure to bring anything important in your case and the rest will be brought to Maine later."

Lily went up to her room and began assessing her belongings. She was a bit concerned about transporting her paintings but decided to wrap them with blankets and other sheets before putting them into the wooden crates her mother set aside for her. Lily didn't own much, but what she did have was special to her. She enjoyed nice things like anyone, but the things that meant the most were meaningless to other people—her shell collection, her books, her letters from Noah. She knew it wasn't practical to put them all in her travel bag so she chose Noah's letters and a paperback copy of Peter Pan—things that would bring her comfort on their travels.

Her last consideration was Noah's painting, which was hanging securely on her wall. She hated to box it up but it didn't seem practical to take it with her. It suddenly dawned on Lily that she didn't even know exactly when they would be leaving. Her parents had not been very specific, just that it would be soon. She heard her mother in the hallway getting ready to head back downstairs so she stopped to ask her.

When Lily opened the door to her bedroom she caught sight of her mother walking through the hall like a ghost. She looked tired and pale. "Mama, when exactly are we moving back to Newland?"

Her mother was obviously distracted for she didn't even notice Lily standing there until she spoke. "First thing tomorrow dear. Now hurry up and pack, there isn't much time."

Lily was completely beside herself. How were they making such a big move so suddenly? It began to dawn on her that she probably wouldn't even have time to inform her teachers or say goodbye to her schoolmates. She thought about the pink pencil case she left in her desk at school. She loved that pencil case and would be sorry to leave it behind. Perhaps it was trivial, but nothing seemed rational at that moment.

It was a long night. Lily and her parents were up until almost dawn packing up the last of their belongings and choosing what to leave behind. Exhausted, Lily collapsed on her soft, stripped bed and drifted off to sleep for an hour before her parents woke her to tell her it was time to go. More than anything she wanted the warmth of a cozy quilt and to wake up from all the confusion.

Not wanting to make things difficult on her parents, Lily managed to drag herself from the room, pulling the strap of her satchel over her head and grabbing the small suitcase that held the necessities for the trip and a few small personal items. She followed her parents down the narrow staircase of the brownstone townhouse one last time, walked out the front door, and was on her way back to Newland. She took one last look at her Boston home, imprinting it in her mind, and closed the book on another chapter of her life. God only knew what was in store for them.

CHAPTER TEN

The blue cottage had laid dormant only a month before it was occupied once again. All the preparations the Stephens family made to secure it for the long winter months were all for naught. Once again it had come alive and was stocked with food in the cupboards, the beds were draped in fresh linens and just now a fire was blazing in the little stone hearth which chased away the early evening chill.

Lily sat on the orange and yellow braided rug near the fire and gazed into the flames, hypnotized by the flickering light. The last few days were a blur. Her family had so quickly made the decision to pack up their belongings and head to Maine that Lily had not yet found the time to process the incredible turn of events. For now, she was content to just sit and unwind with her parents after a long day. They had only arrived that morning, and with all the hustle of getting the home ready for the living, they did not yet have a chance to inform any friends of their arrival. It seemed best to put it off until the next day as they all needed a chance to recuperate and get settled.

The moment of solace didn't last through the night though when suddenly came a soft knock at the door. Lily rose to answer and who should be standing at their threshold but Flora. Flora and Everett Durgin were siblings who lived a couple of houses down that both Lily and Noah considered close friends. Flora was a year younger than Lily and was known to be a bubbly, energetic girl who very much looked up to her older brother. While her bouncy spiral raven curls and frilly frocks were her signature look, she had been somewhat of a tomboy at heart. Lily noticed that summer how that spirit was damped when her brother Everett started an apprenticeship working the shipyards down in Portland.

At the moment Flora wore a look of astonishment on her face at the sight of her dearest friend, Lily. "What are you doing here, Lily?" She exclaimed with high-pitched glee. "I saw smoke coming from your chimney and I just couldn't believe you would be back so soon! Will you be staying long?"

Lily laughed, her own spirits being raised slightly at the girl's enthusiasm. "Oh Flora, you wouldn't believe it, but it looks like we're here to stay."

Flora squealed with delight at the news, not even bothering to ask how or why. "Lily, that is utterly fantastic news!" She hugged her friend tightly. "I can't tell you how lonely it's been around here since you, Noah, and Everett left."

Lily hadn't considered how much the absence of so many loved ones might have affected Flora and for that, she was all the more glad to be back at the blue cottage. She hugged her friend in return and apologized for not having given notice of their arrival. "It all happened rather suddenly," she explained. "Father's job didn't work out and so he decided we should move back at once. I didn't have time to write but was planning to come by and tell you tomorrow. Though I must say how glad it makes me to see you sooner!"

The friends hugged again, and Lily invited Flora to come in from the chilly air. Flora accepted but promised to only stay a short while, not wanting to walk back home in the dark as well as having the impression that Lily and her parents were likely exhausted from their move. Lily went to put on some tea and then joined Flora by the fire.

"The nights are already getting quite a bit colder already," Flora complained. "It's probably the hardest part about living in Maine. When I grow up I am going to move to Florida, like Noah, only I'll never come back. Give me warm weather all year long so that I can walk on the beach and swim in the ocean any time I like!"

Flora's comments struck Lily as she hadn't contemplated until now the possibility that Noah might end up preferring the sub-tropical climate of Florida. She was sure she wouldn't like to live there herself. "Well, I love all the seasons here in the north," she politely retorted. "I don't think I will ever miss Virginia for all its hot and humid weather and drab, rainy winters."

Flora giggled. "I suppose when you put it like that it doesn't sound so appealing after all, but I bet a place like Florida with palm trees and coconuts would be quite intriguing. Did you have palm trees in Virginia?"

Lily was sad to say that there had not been palm trees and somehow that put the issue to rest in Flora's mind that it must be completely different then. Still, both of them had to admit there was something exceptionally cozy about sitting by a warm fire in October, sipping tea, and catching up with a friend.

Flora then began to fill Lily in a bit about what had

been going on in Newland since she left a month ago. Her brother had written recently and said he had so impressed the owner of one of the ship companies that he wanted to take Everett on full time after he finished his apprenticeship. She also informed Lily that Ruth and her boyfriend Wade were inseparable and people expected they would get engaged within the year. Other than that, little had changed but Flora still liked having the first chance to inform Lily of all the recent goings-on and made a point to include her own recent development, which was that she developed a bit of a crush on a boy at school named Tobias who was very sweet despite being a bit shy and awkward. Flora enjoyed teasing him almost as much as he enjoyed her teasing and didn't seem to mind when she called him Toby. He told her she was very pretty once, and Flora received a flower from a secret admirer who she was almost certain was Toby.

"I sure hope it wasn't that horrible Henry Allen," she added with an exasperated tone. "He is mean to all the girls, especially me, but my friend Katrina is convinced he has a big crush on me. I can't say I haven't suspected it as well, but he is such a brute, so he has another thing coming. Also, there is a boy named Claude who has walked me home from school a couple of times. He is very cute and athletic but not as sweet and smart as Toby."

Flora continued on about the kids from school, mostly the boys, and the more she spoke the more Lily was amused by how well she was getting on without her brother. In fact, she was becoming quite a sought-after young lady that many of her peers admired. Flora was outgoing and quite lovable, but just now Lily was no longer able to keep up with her high energy and a yawn escaped her lips.

"Oh Lily, forgive me, you must be so tired." Flora continued, "I am so sorry for chattering on so. We can talk more about such things another time. It's just so great to have you back. It's going to be a lot less lonely with you here and I couldn't be more thrilled about your return." She grabbed Lily's hand just then. "You are like a sister to me Lily, the sister I never had."

The comment caused a warm smile to spread over Lily's sleepy face. She never had a brother or a sister, so Flora's companionship was of great importance to her as well. Of course, she had a sibling on the way, but that development was an enormous surprise to the entire family and a blessing, as Lily's parents were sure they could no longer have children. But Lily was grateful to have a friend closer to her own age nearby. She thanked Flora for coming then walked her to the door. The sun had not gone down completely, so there was still enough light in the sky to lead Flora home if she hurried.

Flora gave Lily one more hug and then went skipping merrily on her way. Despite Flora's visit being an unplanned one, it was just what Lily needed. It lifted her spirits to hear so much of the good things happening in Newland knowing she would be a part of it again. As much as she liked her schoolmates in Boston, she hadn't grown to love them quite like her friends here. Tomorrow was a new day and she had every intention of making the most of it. But first things first, she must pray. Pray for her parents, pray for her friends, pray for guidance, and most of all pray for her beloved Noah. *I wonder what he's doing right now.* She contemplated as she began to ready herself for a peaceful night of sleep. Oh, to wake up in the blue cottage again—this was truly her home!

CHAPTER ELEVEN

Noah was sitting cross-legged on the bow of the sailboat one peaceful evening, sketching in the book Lily gave him as an early birthday present. He had found it to be an extremely useful gift in those quiet moments where he and Conrad sat in silence, sailing on in a southerly direction. He looked up from his work to take in the lowering sun that illuminated the wispy clouds near the horizon. Nightfall would soon come and another productive day at sea would be behind them. Their next stop was Cape May, New Jersey and so far, they were making great time.

Noah set down his sketchbook as he was beginning to

strain his eyes to see the pencil lines as the sky darkened. He continued looking out at the endless sea, reflecting on the past week. He had learned so much more in that time than he had all that summer when he paid Conrad to teach him the basics of sailing. Clearly, the best teaching tool of all was experience. While things had been fairly smooth, there were still a few unexpected events, including another minor squall as they passed Cape Cod which caused a tear on the mainsail that they had mended promptly in Newport, and they nearly lost their way through a thick fog the prior evening as they prepared to dock in Atlantic City. But otherwise, their voyage was easygoing and fortunately, no hurricanes were being reported on the coast as commonly took place that time of year.

For now, the sea was gently lapping against the ship at the behest of the soft breeze blowing over the surface. Conrad seemed to be in quiet contemplation as he often was in the evening. For all of his usual chatter and flair for dramatic storytelling, Noah realized he actually knew very little about Conrad's former life. He never spoke of family, his childhood, or anything from his past prior to when he began sailing. Noah was initially content to let him share those details in his own time, but after spending so much time together he began to wonder about it more and more.

Noah himself was willing to talk openly about his past

when it came up. He told Conrad about how his mother had died of pneumonia when he was only an infant and how his father had run from facing the pain of her death and left him in the care of his Aunt Prissy. He told him about how his Aunt Prissy was an over-protective guardian who kept him sheltered for the first seventeen years of his life and how little he had known of the world before their sailing adventure, except what he read in books. And he also told him in great detail how Lily came into his life and rescued him from a life of solitude. How fortunate he had been on the day of her arrival and that she would see such potential in him. Aside from his art tutor, Miss Weathervane, no one had ever believed in him or pushed him beyond his comfort zone.

Conrad would often listen with careful interest as Noah spoke of his relationship with Lily. He never said much except that she sounded like a great girl and to "hold onto that one", but Noah sensed an underlying sorrow in his tone, though he hesitated to ask why. This evening Noah was determined to make an attempt to persuade Conrad to break his silence. If for no other reason than to have something new and interesting to talk about. He put his sketchbook in his pocket and took a seat near Conrad at the Captain's wheel.

For the most part, Conrad was an admirable man. He was kind and patient with Noah, made friends easily wherever he went, was honest in his trading, and showed great respect for his craft through hard work and being a responsible captain when at sea. However, once on land Noah was often startled to see some of these commendable traits cast aside in favor of an unpredictable, roguish fellow with a taste for hard liquor. His erratic behavior in this state caused Noah to feel unsettled at times. He still hadn't shaken the unnerving episode in Boston, having to flee for their lives due to a temporary lapse in judgment on Conrad's part. It left him feeling hyper-vigilant at every port to brace himself for any possible drama.

At the moment, Conrad was the picture of serenity and couldn't be further from calamity. "How much further before we reach Cape May?" Noah asked casually.

"About two more hours. We won't get into port until after dark, but it should be early enough to grab a bite to eat before calling it a night."

Noah was glad at that as he was growing weary of the bland meals onboard which consisted mostly of salty meats and stale bread. He wanted a fresh-cooked meal. "We're making good time," he observed. "Are we going to stay for only one night?"

"I was thinking maybe two. There is an old friend I'd like to stop in and see who runs a small inn. He owes me a little money and so I'm going to see if I can collect. It's also a nice little seaside town, I think you'll enjoy taking in the sights."

Not having stopped anywhere for more than one night since Boston, Noah was feeling a little restless and looking forward to spending some time onshore, in spite of Conrad's unpredictable behavior on land. "Sounds good. I always look forward to meeting any friend of yours. You always seem to know the most fascinating people."

Conrad nervously chuckled and said, "Yeah, I do know my share of colorful characters." He then became quiet for a moment and replied offhandedly, "Well, I don't think you'll get a chance to meet this friend of mine. The thing is, he is a busy man, and uh, I just need to pop in to say hello, grab the money and go. I'll probably have you wait for me in town."

Noah found his response curious as he was normally excited to introduce Noah to his friends and this is where the storytelling began. He wondered what made this one different. He wasn't really convinced of the reason Conrad gave about him being "busy" since there was no way of knowing that for sure. Perhaps this was his opening. "Hey Conrad, speaking of old friends, ya know you've never mentioned where you're from. Where did you grow up?"

Conrad fell silent once again before speaking. "I grew up on the coast of Louisiana."

Noah was certain he never heard him mention Louisiana in any capacity and wondered why. "Do you have family there still?"

Conrad answered simply, "Yes."

"Do you have any plans to visit on our trip this winter?"

"No, not this time."

It was clear by his short, flat answers that Conrad wanted the conversation to stagnate, but Noah pressed on. "So, what family do you have back home? Are your parents still living?"

Conrad was irritated now and snapped a little. "Yes, from what I know my mama and daddy are still living. What's with all the questions?"

Noah shrugged, "I dunno, I guess I just wondered why you never talk about it. I just wanted to know a little more about where you come from. Do you have any siblings?"

"None worth mentioning." Conrad's anger was increasing with each passing moment. "Look Noah," he finally barked. "I really don't want to have this discussion right now. It's getting late in the day and I'm tired. Can we change the subject?" Noah had clearly hit on a sore spot, which he was curious to better understand, but knew that now was not the time. He did not want to further upset his friend and mentor so instead he asked a little more about Cape May which suited Conrad just fine.

CHAPTER TWELVE

The *Serenade* pulled into Cape May, New Jersey as scheduled. It was a moonless night and therefore the inky black sky was lit only by the scattering of a trillion stars. The earth absorbed almost none of its light, so aside from the harbor lights and a few warmly lit homes and shops, nothing could be seen from the boat.

As soon as they finished docking, Noah and Conrad headed out quickly hoping to find somewhere inviting for a bit of dinner. They came upon a cozy seaside inn that was going to be closing up soon, but the owner offered to let his cook heat up some leftover clam chowder for the two famished men.

They ate the meal quickly and left with their bellies full and satisfied. Conrad had a glass of whiskey but seemed to be holding it well.

The more time Conrad spent with Noah the less inhibited he was regarding his drinking. The truth was, he wanted to set a good example for the young lad but didn't have the strength to resist a stiff drink when given the chance. The best he could do was refrain from offering him a drink of his own, which was challenging as no one likes to drink alone. But Conrad had seen strong drink take hold of too many good men and he never wanted to be responsible for introducing it to Noah should it become all-consuming for him as well. It was an all too easy remedy for boredom for men at sea.

Most men enjoyed a drink or two so Noah didn't think much of Conrad's proclivity for alcohol unless he became unreasonably intoxicated, which he usually hid by staying out late or holing himself up in his cabin. Conrad was a man's man, so there was nothing unusual about his social drinking. If anything, Noah felt a tad self-conscious for the fact that he didn't have any experience with it. Many boys his age had already developed a taste for liquor but his lack of exposure to it kept him from indulging. Perhaps he was even a little frightened at the prospect of turning to it as an escape from the pain of losing his father or when he was missing Lily terribly. Whatever the reason, he had thus far refrained from indulging his curiosity.

After dinner, Conrad wanted to head immediately back to the boat to catch some sleep. He planned to be up early to visit his friend and in truth, that was one of the reasons he only indulged in one glass of whiskey. He needed to be sharp and sober for the task ahead of him. So bright and early, before Noah even awoke, he was on his way, leaving a note saying he would be back before noon.

Noah decided to head into town and take a stroll through the market to scare up some breakfast. It was a little bit of a trek which gave Noah the chance to take in the fresh air and stretch his legs a bit. The town was quaint and lined with a neat row of trees, already bursting with reds and oranges, and freshly planted mums to match. Fallen leaves were strewn about the streets, which gathered along the buildings when a gust of wind blew them about. The townsfolk were dressed in heavy knit turtleneck sweaters, lightweight overcoats and colorful scarves tied loosely around their necks.

The locals seemed content with the diminished crowd of the morning at the end of a busy summer season once packed with beachgoers from out of town. Noah enjoyed looking through the sweetly decorated shop windows and was drawn by the smell of freshly baked bread wafting from a nearby bakery. He went in and grabbed a warm roll, some fresh fruit, and a steaming cup of black coffee then had a seat on a bench outside. He watched a woman opening a floral shop across the street, setting out fresh bouquets for sale, and thought how much he would love to buy one for Lily if she were with him just now. He also watched another gentleman who owned a bookstore stacking a table with leatherbound classics.

After finishing his breakfast, Noah walked over to the little bookstore and flipped through the pile of books. Most of the titles he had read and the ones he hadn't didn't interest him much. He then continued walking down the street, stopping briefly at the floral shop to admire a perfect white lily which made him think of his beloved once again. She was ever-present in his thoughts but just now his heart ached with missing her.

Soon Noah was passing a jewelry store that he almost overlooked, but a glint of silver caught his eye in the window. On display was the most stunning sterling silver pendant of a sailboat set on a crested wave hanging from a simple, silver chain. He went inside to take a closer look. The owner of the shop was friendly and eager to assist Noah since he was the only customer in view. He didn't need convincing though. He purchased the necklace immediately, the shop owner placed it gently in a navy, velvet-lined box and wrapped it up for shipping. Noah filled out a card with Lily's address and the man assured him the item would be shipped off to Boston that very afternoon.

The impetuous purchase pleased Noah tremendously. Perhaps it was unwise to spend such an extravagant sum so early in his trip, but he could think of no better way to remind Lily of how much she captivated his heart and how he was thinking of her each step of the journey. He never wanted to lose sight of the fact that she was the reason he was able to do this at all. He owed her an incredible debt of gratitude and therefore it was worth every penny.

He spent the rest of his morning wandering through town and then scoping out the waterfront. He watched as other sailboats floated by in the distance and wondered where they might be headed to. He so enjoyed his time that he didn't even realize it was past noon, then began to head back to the boat so Conrad didn't worry about him. He stopped at a market on his way out to stock up on a few food supplies for the next leg of the journey and then trotted back to the marina.

It was nearly one o'clock and Noah fully expected to see Conrad waiting for him, but the boat was empty. There was no sign that Conrad had returned and no note, so Noah decided to pull out his sketchbook and finish his drawing from the night before as he waited for his friend. Once the sketch was completed Noah felt a little drowsy from being out in the sun, so he headed into his cabin and drifted off to sleep for a bit. When he awoke, he found he had slept longer than he planned and that it was getting late in the day, but still no sign of Conrad.

Hours passed and it was now nearing nightfall. Noah was becoming deeply concerned. Whereas earlier he told himself he probably lost track of time catching up with an old friend, he now began to recall once again the trouble Conrad found himself in during their time in Boston and worst-case scenarios began to play out in his mind. He contemplated whether or not he should go looking for him, but he didn't even know where to begin. He knew nothing about the friend Conrad went to see except that he ran a small inn. That wasn't much to go on, but it was something.

Noah had just about made his mind up to contact the local authorities and begin his search when he saw Conrad stumbling up the marina, shouting Noah's name. He seemed to have forgotten where he docked the boat, and it didn't take long to figure out why. Noah hopped out of the boat to assist his confused friend and as he drew closer it became quite obvious he was drunk. There was also a blood stain streaming from his nose and his right eye was puffy and blue. It appeared he had been in a fight after all.

Noah was prepared to flee the scene once again, as they did in Boston, but before he could reach Conrad and lead him to the boat, Conrad stumbled over his own feet and fell sideways into the harbor. Due to the yelling and splashing Conrad made while flailing his arms around, other boaters began to emerge to see what the commotion was. Noah didn't hesitate to jump in after him and was able to lead him safely to a ladder so they could climb their way out. Conrad fell back a couple of times in his pathetic attempt to hoist himself out of the harbor, but with Noah following behind as a guide he finally made it out safe and sound.

Noah looked upon the crowd and called out sheepishly, "Everything's okay, I got him." So slowly the other boaters ambled back to their own cabins as the best part of the show was now over. Once back on *The Serenade*, Noah quickly found a wool blanket and wrapped Conrad in it who was now shivering, but still a ways from sobering up despite his impromptu dive into the cold ocean water.

Uncertain what to do next, Noah tried reasoning with Conrad to get an idea of how imminent his danger might still be. "Is everything okay Conrad," he yelled, "Do we need to head out?"

Conrad smiled foolishly, "No, we're fine. All is fine. Except it never really will be again." He was frowning now. "Who cares about anything. She's gone. Yup, gone for good. Who cares? She didn't love me. She never loved me. Just let me sleep. I just need to sleep. That's all…" And with that he laid down on the bench seat and began snoring loudly. Noah figured this was not an urgent situation, so he covered Conrad once again with the wool blanket and let him sleep it off.

CHAPTER THIRTEEN

Conrad was busying himself with boat maintenance when Noah got up the next morning, preparing *The Serenade* to head out for another day at sea. Despite drinking heavily the night before, Conrad was still the first to rise and get the day started. Noah made a silent vow to himself that he would make an effort in the days ahead to be up before Conrad, at least occasionally, to show his willingness to work just as hard.

Noah said a polite good morning and Conrad simply nodded his head in acknowledgment. After helping him change out a few chafed lines, Noah finally spoke. "About last night…"

"Look kid, I really don't think we need to discuss it."

"I think we do, Conrad." Noah boldly continued, "You came back so much later than you said you would, and I wasn't sure I'd be able to find you if something went wrong."

"Well, I was fine kid, so don't worry about it, okay?"

"What about next time? What if you were in trouble? What am I supposed to do?"

Conrad did not appreciate this line of questioning. "I'll tell you what you do—man up and figure it out. I don't answer to you or anyone for that matter. I'm not your daddy. I live by my own rules and I can't concern myself with your wellbeing too."

Noah was visibly hurt by that comment. As much as he knew Conrad to be a loner, Noah still thought there was a mutual affinity between them and in truth, Conrad was the only man in his life who he looked up to. But the words also stung because it was a callous reminder that his own father was dead, and that once again, he had no one to count on.

Conrad immediately regretted the thoughtless remark. "I'm sorry kid, I really am, it's just, I'm in no position to be responsible for another person. When we're at sea, as long as I'm the captain it is my first and foremost duty to get you back to land safely, but when we're out here in the real world. Well,

I just can't make any promises. I'm not your guy."

Noah looked away, lowering his voice he replied, "I get it, Conrad. I'm just another passenger on your boat, but the truth is, our friendship is important to me. You've taught me everything I know. And yes, it would be unreasonable for me to expect you to always take me into consideration in everything you do, but remember, you're all I have out here and if something happened to you, well, I just never considered until today what I would do."

Conrad felt deeply ashamed. He didn't want to show it just then, but it had been a long time since he actually cared for another human being besides himself. He also knew he was weak and had too many troubles to be anyone's mentor and did not feel worthy of such an honor.

"I'm sorry Noah, honestly. I will try to be more mindful of these things in the future, but I just can't make any promises. You have to understand how it's been for me all these years. I'm used to going it alone without answering to anybody and it's a rough life out here at sea. Maybe it was a mistake to have you come along..."

"No, it was not a mistake," Noah said emphatically. "This has been the greatest experience of my life and I have you to thank. You have taught me so much and I have no right to ask for more than that. You are right, I need to take responsibility for myself. Let's just forget the whole thing."

Conrad nodded in agreement and the two finished getting the boat ready to ship off. The whole incident blew over quickly as neither man wanted to hold a grudge. More than anything Noah was thankful that nothing serious happened last night and they were on their way once again, back in the open sea, sails flapping wildly and heading toward their next destination. And despite Conrad's effort to lower Noah's expectations of him, nothing had changed. Noah believed in Conrad and suspected there was more to his erratic behavior than meets the eyes and hoped to one day better understand what it was.

Life in Newland was an easy adjustment for Lily. She loved the blue cottage by the sea and all the people she knew. The hardest part was not having Noah there to share in her joy. The day after her family got settled Lily took a walk on her own along the shore and found herself standing before Birchwood Cottage, just like she did the first day she and

Noah met. It seemed like a lifetime ago when she considered how much had taken place since that moment.

She stood looking at the empty house which seemed dark and sad somehow. She shivered at the eeriness though one might think it was due to the cool ocean air. How much she longed to one day call Birchwood Cottage home. She took note of the windows to Aunt Prissy's old sitting room and thought about Noah's remark that he hoped one day to build them a painting studio in there. She could see it all quite clearly in her mind and wondered if that day would ever come. For now, it seemed a long time off.

After her walk on the beach, Lily decided to head into town and pay a visit to some friends. She first stopped to say hello to Aunt Prissy and her new husband, Buck Simmons. They were of course surprised to see her, but glad to hear she would be saying indefinitely. Aunt Prissy gave her a warm embrace. Though Lily and Aunt Prissy had not always seen eye to eye regarding Noah's care, that was all water under the bridge. There was no question in either of their minds that they both loved Noah deeply and being together again made him seem closer somehow.

"You must see my new garden!" Aunt Prissy said with much enthusiasm, "Thankfully we have not had too much of a frost to kill all the flowers off yet."

Lily was glad to entertain the suggestion as she was always impressed with Priscilla's gardening skills and took great interest in seeing what she'd been up to in her new home. Buck's late wife had been sick for many years and was not capable of tending to the yard much, and Buck himself often joked of his own black thumb, so the transformation was quite astonishing for so short a time. Lily gasped with delight over the bright daylilies, the sweet columbines, the cheery hollyhocks, the lush hydrangeas, and the rich fragrance emanating from the English roses. "You must teach me more of your secrets someday," she gushed and Aunt Prissy was all too happy to accommodate her wish by promising to stop by in the spring and show her a few tips. Lily also desired to keep up with the garden at Birchwood Cottage to surprise Noah when he came home. Aunt Prissy agreed to work on it together, which was a huge progression in their relationship as Priscilla was known to be quite possessive of such things.

After catching up a bit more, Lily headed further into town to call on Reverend Thomas, his wife, and their daughters Ruth and Leah. Mrs. Thomas answered the door and invited Lily in with much delight at seeing the young girl. Leah sat quietly in a chair set in the corner of the sitting room, rocking back and forth adamantly. Ruth sat on the sofa working on a quilt for an upcoming craft show at the church where they were raising money for a new wood stove for the widow Hamilton before winter.

Ruth got up quickly and hugged her friend. She too was surprised by her sudden return to Newland but was genuinely glad to see her. At one time Lily wasn't so sure Ruth would still be eager to remain friends as Ruth had fallen in love with Noah. Though he tried to give Ruth a chance, Noah's heart belonged only to Lily and eventually, he had no choice but to be honest about his feelings. Ruth's heart was broken so the two parted on poor terms, but now all seemed forgiven. Helping her to nurse her heart back to health was Wade Anderson, a boy she met in church who doted on Ruth endlessly.

The truth was, Ruth did envy Lily's captivating personality and naturally sunny disposition, but as with most people, she truly liked her and was proud to call her a friend. Ruth herself was a striking redhead who was growing more beautiful with each passing year but even coupled with her pleasant demeanor she could not compete with Lily in Noah's eyes. It took Ruth a while to get over the disappointment, as she always had her sights set on him, but his love for Lily was so evident she came to accept it in time.

"My goodness Lily, it's so good to see you! Such great news that you're planning to stay with us for good." Ruth said enthusiastically, "I'll bet Noah is just thrilled."

"Actually, he doesn't know yet," Lily replied nervously. "He came to see me on his way down through Boston, but he had to go unexpectedly, or else he would have been there to hear the news. I won't be able to inform him of what's going on until he gets to Florida."

Ruth was surprised to hear Noah didn't know yet. "Well, I wonder if he'll turn right back around knowing you're in Newland. It seems the only reason he left was that he figured you'd be down in Boston for your final year of school. What do you think he'll do?"

Lily hadn't considered that. "I will definitely encourage him to continue on his travels. Nothing has changed. I still have to focus on my studies and he needs this time for himself."

Ruth was impressed with Lily's unselfish attitude but wondered if in the end, she would relent. "Well, I can tell you without question, Wade would not be willing to leave my side for anything in the world." She knew it was mean to make that statement, as it was so against her character to ever be unkind, but she did take some small satisfaction in knowing her man was nearby and she didn't have to suffer seeing Noah with Lily for a while. Even though she hated to admit it, she still held a minor grudge, though she attempted to cast it aside.

Lily picked up on Ruth's self-satisfied tone and decided to ignore it out of pity. "I don't mind," she reassured her. "I think this trip is exactly what Noah needs. He really loves sailing and deserves a little adventure after all those years cooped up at Birchwood Cottage."

Ruth couldn't argue with that and instead changed the topic. "I know you just got back to town and all, but you must come have dinner with us one of these nights. Oh Lily, and you simply must get to know Wade. I know the two of you briefly met this summer, but I think you'll enjoy his company, he is such a dear. Please say you can arrange it soon. I'll even invite Flora if you'd like."

A night out with some people her own age sounded incredibly appealing. "I'd love that, Ruth. Anytime that suits you works for me. After all, I just got back into town, so my social calendar is pretty much wide open right now."

The two girls laughed and Ruth continued talking about all the other upcoming events that Lily wouldn't want to miss. They then set a date for dinner the following week and before heading out, Lily stopped to talk to Reverend Thomas and his wife who informed her that they would look for her in church Sunday. Yes, easing back into her life in Newland was going to be simple indeed.

CHAPTER FOURTEEN

A few days had passed without incident and things between Noah and Conrad were pretty much back to normal as they settled into their routine at sea. Noah found a lot of time to think on those long days of travel as Conrad wasn't really in a talkative mood. He also spent some of his downtime sketching and reading. He brought along a handful of books, including his favorite pocket book of poetry, Captains Courageous by Rudyard Kipling, Two Years Before the Mast by Richard Henry Dana, his well-worn copy of Peter Pan, and a Bible.

Noah didn't grow up being very religious. While his

Aunt Prissy didn't show any disdain for God at all, she did often make disparaging remarks about the church and even Reverend Thomas. Things had changed considerably since that time and now Aunt Prissy and Reverend Thomas were friends, but she still held some cynical views when it came to "religious folk." Noah believed in God and was always fascinated with the stories in the Bible, especially great tales like David and Goliath, Samson and Delilah, or Daniel in the lion's den, but had never really thought much more about it until he started attending Reverend Thomas's services.

He was now far more interested in the Bible and would spend his morning pouring over the scriptures. He was learning a lot about the man he wanted to be and even began praying more, something Lily talked about often. It was a little unusual at first, talking to someone you couldn't see, but he eventually began to find a great deal of comfort knowing that even when he was alone that God was keeping watch over him and cared for his wellbeing. At night he would often lay near the bow of the boat, look up at the brilliant array of stars in the sky and speak to God. Tonight, his prayer was simple.

God, thank you for all you've done for me. Thank you for making our journey smooth these past few days. Thank you for bringing Lily into my life. Please watch over her and her family while I'm away. Keep her safe. Help her with her studies and let her know she is loved. Thank you for all you've done for my Aunt Prissy and that you brought her a good husband to care for her. And God, please be with Conrad. Give him wisdom as captain of this boat and help him with whatever troubles he may be experiencing. And help me to be a good friend and a hard worker. Guide my steps and my future. Amen.

Just as he completed his silent prayer Conrad spoke. "Tomorrow we should reach the Carolinas. Looks like there may be some rain and wind ahead, so I was thinking we could take some of the Intracoastal Waterway to get a break from the rough seas." He then asked Noah to take the wheel while he headed down to his cabin to grab an evening snack.

Conrad had been letting Noah take the wheel more frequently now and he wondered if he'd let him navigate through the waterway too. It would be a great experience. Conrad felt he was a natural and had great instincts, which boosted Noah's confidence. More and more he dreamed of being the captain of his own sailboat someday. Above all, he would often daydream of taking Lily on their own private voyages, as she was sure to share in his passion for sailing. Her disposition and thirst for adventure were perfectly suited for it.

Tomorrow would be a new undertaking. Noah liked the idea of seeing land again. He wondered how long before he'd see palm trees, a sure sign that they were nearing their final destination. *It won't be long now*, he thought to himself. *This time next week I should be looking at a tropical paradise.*

That evening was Lily's dinner engagement with the Thomas's. She was very much looking forward to an evening out and Flora was eager to accompany her. "Oh my goodness," she cried. "I've been wanting an excuse to wear my new dress!"

Lily laughed knowing that Flora had several new dresses she was eager to show off. Now that Everett was off working in Portland, her parents poured all their affection into their little girl and she wanted for nothing. Flora was undoubtedly spoiled, and perhaps a little stupid, but she was never conceited. No, she was in fact uncommonly friendly to everyone she came in contact with. She couldn't help her nature to enjoy pretty things, but she was too unrefined to act snobbish.

They walked over to the Thomas's house together. Lily was herself wearing a new sage green dress with gold accents and feeling pretty. Her hair was pinned in a loose updo with soft strands of curls framing her rosy face. Flora's hair was down in her usual tight ringlets, but each side adorned with little bows for effect. She looked like a porcelain doll.

The air was cool, so they covered their shoulders with warm wraps that they hugged tightly around their shoulders. The smell of burning wood wafted from the chimney tops and colored leaves blanketed their path. They trotted along happily in anticipation of a pleasant evening, talking of nothing in particular.

They arrived in a timely manner and were invited in to have a seat at the large mahogany table in the dining room. Ruth and Leah were already seated, awaiting their guests, along with Wade who played the part of the perfect gentleman, rising to pull out the chairs for all the young ladies. Wade was a peculiar-looking fellow. He had a curly mop of auburn hair and a rather generous nose that was splashed with light freckles. His smile was his winning feature and made him look attractive despite his unconventional looks.

While he and Lily met once for only a moment, she was looking forward to getting to know him better. It sounded like he treated Ruth very well and she spoke highly of his intelligence and wit. Indeed, the first thing he said once he sat down was a clever remark about how much he was looking forward to enjoying a meal in such lovely company and that he should never want to go back to breaking bread among common people again.

In truth, they were common people, but tonight Wade took it upon himself to make them feel like royalty by offering to serve them personally. While Wade could be a serious sort of boy, he had a quirky sense of humor which allowed him to cut loose tonight and play the ass. It was clear that he did not take his role too seriously as he spoke in an exaggerated French accent as he brought each plate of food out to Ruth and her friends.

He was dressed to impress and draped a napkin over his arm for effect. "S'il vous plait Mademoiselle, what would you like to drink?" He asked Lily in a convincing French accent.

"What are ze options?" She replied, in her own comical attempt to play along.

"Water, juice, or tea?"

"Tea if you please Monsieur, with sugar," she answered.

"Oui, oui, if it pleases Mademoiselle." He bowed then turned to Flora and asked the same.

"Ooh juice please, kind sir!" She squealed, clapping her hands in excitement at the little game.

Leah was silent as usual, but her eyes widened when

Wade spoke to her as if she'd never seen such a ridiculous person. "She'll take water," Ruth said pointedly.

Leah sat down next to Lily by choice. Though she didn't interact with other people much, she seemed content in Lily's presence. Lily always went out of her way to include Leah in any group setting, even if only complimenting a bit of sewing she had done or remarking on the books she had on her shelf. It's not that Leah was unfriendly by choice, but she had what the doctors said was a brain issue that left her with little desire to interact with others. Her family were the only ones who knew how to communicate with her to find out what pleased her, but the fact that she didn't shirk Lily's hugs was proof enough that she was acceptable in Leah's eyes.

Wade moved onto Ruth, to whom he presented a perfect red rose. "Ze flower for ma belle," he said continuing his exaggerated French accent.

Ruth blushed as she took it from his hands. "Why thank you, it's very pretty," she beamed and then asked for some tea. She didn't play along beyond that, in part because she didn't really understand how to partake in those kinds of games. Ruth was a sweet, but simple girl. She was rarely the center of attention so receiving the rose in front of all her friends made the night special enough.

Wade continued to wait on the girls until the entrée

came out, which was breathtakingly arrayed and consisted of grilled pork chops, roasted potatoes, and a medley of squash and zucchini. They each commented on how delicious the meal looked. Wade reclaimed his seat among the girls as they returned to being themselves.

"So, Ruth tells me you are a painter," Wade said to Lily, trying to make polite conversation.

"Well, I don't know if I would call myself a painter, but I do paint, yes. I'm not nearly as good as our friend Noah. He is a true artist." Lily often undercut her own talents while singing the praises of others.

"Oh, don't be so modest," Ruth responded, slightly annoyed by Lily's humble response.

Wade continued without noticing. "Yes, rumor has it this Noah is well on his way to becoming a master painter. I studied classical art last year and found it fascinating, but I don't paint a lick."

Lily enjoyed the fact that Noah's reputation preceded him. "He has helped me improve a great deal, though it is more of a hobby for me. I do enjoy it immensely. What is it you do for fun, Wade?"

Wade smiled brightly now. "Glad you asked. I hope to be a chef someday."

"He made our meal tonight," Ruth interjected proudly.

"That was to be a secret, my dear Ruth," he said with a wink and a hint of false humility.

Both Lily and Flora were impressed. As silly as his presentation was, it was clear he took his culinary skills seriously as everything was both beautiful and tasty. Ruth beamed once again, this time with pride for Wade's accomplishment.

The evening was an overall success and the company was enjoyed by all. Lily and Flora walked home together after nightfall, laughing and chattering once again, practicing their French accents and talking about how much they wished Noah and Everett had been there. Lily knew Flora didn't like to walk home in the dark, so she walked her over to her house first before heading home.

Lily was in a light mood as she started up the path of her own home when she heard noises coming from just outside the house. All the lights were on inside and her mother was wailing. Lily approached to find a police officer standing by the doorway and her father being led out with his hands restrained behind his back.

"Papa, what is going on?" She cried out in confusion at the scene before her. "Where are they taking you?"

Her father's head hung low. "Your mother will explain everything sweetheart, please just go inside."

"I don't understand," she continued.

Her mother pleaded through her tears. "Please honey, do as your father says and go inside. We'll talk later."

Lily hesitated, wishing to put up a fight for once, but was compelled by the anguished look in her mother's eyes to do as she was told. She couldn't understand why her father was being taken away and felt treated like a child in being banished from the scene. She stepped into the entryway and took one last look at her father before closing the door. A short time later her mother came in the house, her face streaked with tears and a look of deep sorrow.

"Your father is in trouble Lily, please pray. Pray harder than you ever have before!" She said before breaking down into uncontrolled sobs.

CHAPTER FIFTEEN

Lily was scared. Her mother cried for almost an hour straight and she still didn't know what was going on and why her father was arrested. She waited as patiently as she could, pacing the floor of her bedroom, anxious for an explanation, and doing her best to remain calm.

It had been almost two weeks since they left their home in Boston and Lily was so focused on settling into life in Newland that she forgot all about the distressed nature in which her parents fled the city. She wondered if there was some correlation as her father hadn't been up to much since they moved back into the blue cottage. Perhaps a bit on edge, but Lily chalked it up to the need to take some time to settle his nerves after all that transpired.

A few moments later she heard her mother knock lightly on her bedroom door. Lily opened it and was shocked by her appearance. Never had her mother looked so utterly pathetic. Her face was blotchy and her eyes red from crying and she was still trembling. She hugged her belly as if grasping for anything to keep her sane. She was so large with child now.

"Please mama, tell me what's going on with papa, I can't bear to wait another minute," Lily begged.

"My dear, sweet girl," her mother whispered. "Your father…lost track of a large sum of money at the office in Boston. They are accusing him of stealing it."

Lily waited to hear if there was more to the story, but her mother was stone silent. "Well, did he take it?" She finally asked, dreading the answer.

Her mother looked down. "He says he didn't, but I'm not sure. There are a lot of unexplained things. That's why we had to leave Boston so quickly. I don't know what we're going to do if your father goes to jail. And me, having a baby soon." Tears started to well up in her eyes once more.

Lily put her arm around her mother and comforted her. "Mama don't worry, we're going to be alright. You have me and we have friends here. You don't need to be afraid.

Papa couldn't have done this thing he's accused of. He's always been so good and upright. Everything will be fine, you'll see. He just needs to explain it and will be home in no time."

Lily's mother rested her head on her daughter's shoulder. "Oh, I do hope you're right, honey. Your father has always taken care of us. I am terribly frightened for us and for him. You know your father; he isn't strong like you."

It was Lily's turn to shed tears. She didn't feel strong at the moment. But as much as she always looked up to her father, her mother was right. He was a docile and sensitive soul. There was no way he could handle a life behind bars. She couldn't imagine her father had taken the money. He was always one to set a good example for his family, being responsible and teaching the importance of honesty. How could it be so?

There wasn't much more they could do that night. Lily reassured her mother once again that they would get through everything together, then helped her to bed before going to lay down herself. As she stared up at the ceiling, she thought of Noah. Once again, she wished he was there with her—he would make sure she and her mother were taken care of. For the first time, she really started to think that maybe she had been mistaken to encourage him to go on his trip after all. Now she would have to wait to hear from him before she could fill him in on how much trouble the Stephens family had gotten themselves into. As she struggled to fall asleep it occurred to her that it might be a good idea to visit Reverend Thomas in the morning to see what he thought of the situation. The idea gave her enough peace to drift off in spite of all the unanswered questions that still loomed large in her mind.

The visit with Reverend Thomas was as fruitful as Lily could hope. She stopped by the church bright and early and found him in his study doing his daily devotionals as he prepared for Sunday's sermon. "What can I do for you, Lily?" he asked kindly, offering her a seat in a leather armchair across from his large mahogany desk. After taking note of the dining table the other night one thing was clear—Reverend Thomas liked mahogany.

Lily always considered Reverend Thomas to be a friendly, but formal man which was reflected in his study. There was a scent in the room of light musk. The walls were lined in bookshelves containing miscellaneous books and volumes on theology and other philosophical thought. The books were so neatly arrayed that Lily thought they looked as though they were never actually read but displayed for effect. In the spaces not taken up by bookshelves there were perfectly placed framed paintings of well-known fathers of the faith—Martin Luther, John Wesley, and George Whitfield. On the desk itself, his leather Bible laid open to the book of Luke, and a small leatherbound cup held five or six various writing utensils, including one topped with a feather.

"Reverend Thomas, I am coming to you in the hopes that I trust our conversation will remain confidential."

"Well, that all depends, my dear, are you in trouble of some sort? You are a minor person, and it would be my duty to inform your father and mother of anything that might be their right to know."

Lily shifted in her seat, unsure if she should continue. "It's just that…it's actually *concerning* my mother and father. They don't know I'm here but I'm worried for them and need some advice."

"Hmm," Reverend Thomas rubbed his chin as he considered his answer. "I'll tell you what, as long as what you tell me doesn't involve you being compromised in any manner, I'm sure I could be depended on as a confidant."

That was all the encouragement Lily needed to spill her guts. She explained the whole sordid mess about why they moved back to Newland, her father's arrest, and now her concern for her mother who was frightened and soon to give birth. "I don't know if she or the baby can handle the stress of the situation. She is greatly worried about how we will manage without my father to care for us and how it will look for our family if he has to stand trial."

The Reverend listened closely to all Lily shared and frowned deeply as she explained their plight. "I'm so sorry my dear, this is an awful circumstance you and your mother find yourselves in. It is for God and the law to judge whether or not your father is guilty and if he will be condemned of committing any crimes, but that does not mean the innocent should suffer. Let me talk to Mrs. Thomas and see how we might be able to help should you need some assistance. You will certainly not want for food or clothing. And what about Noah? I have heard you are engaged to be married. Have you notified him of your plight?"

"No sir," Lily said quietly. "I haven't received word of where he may be reached just yet. He is still at sea from what I gather."

"That is concerning," Reverend Thomas said shaking his head, "It's unfortunate when capable young men want to shirk their duties and leave home to go gallivanting to unknown lands and among who knows what kind of questionable characters. There is no accountability in it."

Lily was quick to defend her beloved. "Reverend Thomas, please do not be so hard on Noah. He went on this trip with both mine and his Aunt Prissy's blessing. You know how long he was cooped up at Birchwood Cottage and what he went through with the loss of his father. This was an opportunity for him to make up for lost time and pursue his passion for sailing. In fact, I'm not so sure I would even want him to know what's going on because he would put an end to his trip in an instant if he knew we were in trouble. He will be back soon enough; we just need enough help to sustain us 'til then."

The Reverend nodded and stood up to show Lily out. "All will be well, dear girl. In Newland, we always take care of our own and you and your mother have nothing to fear. I will talk things over with my wife, as I said, and will be in touch."

Lily hesitated before leaving. "Just give me time to explain our conversation to my mother and please tell Mrs. Thomas to also keep our circumstance confidential for the time being as I don't believe my mother could handle it becoming public knowledge so soon. At least not before she's had a chance to speak to my father and find out if there will be any charges against him."

Reverend Thomas reassured her once again that she had nothing to concern herself with and that he would not share the information with anyone besides his wife. Lily left feeling better knowing that she and her mother would not be alone should they need some support and assistance. She was certain there would have been no one to turn to in Boston for such help and once again she was grateful to be back in Newland.

CHAPTER SIXTEEN

In spite of their expectation for rain, the most precipitation Conrad and Noah experienced was a bit of light drizzle. Fog was the far bigger threat to their travels as they struggled to stay on course as they headed for the Carolinas. Their entrance to the Intracoastal Waterway was just south of the Virginia and North Carolina border and Conrad didn't want to miss it. Thankfully they didn't drift too far off course and before they knew it, the fog began to clear up and land could be seen in the distance once again. They followed it closely so as not to pass the opening between Hatteras and Nags Head.

Conrad remarked that now they would have an easy go of it and the clouds in the distance spelled mild weather ahead. The days were getting shorter, but the temperatures were warming the further south they went. Noah enjoyed spending most of the last couple evenings on deck, gazing at the stars and contemplating the meaning of life. Never had he felt so small as he did on those dark, quiet nights on the vast ocean. The profundity of prayer to an omnipresent God was never more evident.

Things had changed a bit between Conrad and Noah since they left New Jersey. Conrad had slipped into a morose state of being. It was different from both the laidback style Noah was accustomed to and his more untamed behavior. It wasn't that he was unfriendly or cold, but it appeared as though mentally he were a million miles away.

Noah felt it was best to leave him to his contemplations after his unsuccessful attempt to get him to open up earlier on. He began to think that perhaps men didn't talk about their private thoughts and feelings. Noah still had a lot to learn, and for the most part, just concentrated on taking orders and remaining neutral. Even his own ramblings about Lily and all the people back in Newland had subsided. Noah decided it was probably best not to bring those things up unless asked, which Conrad rarely did. Noah didn't even make a comment as they passed Virginia about how Lily was originally from there, instead, he confided those observations to himself.

Even still, the travel was not unpleasant. On the contrary, they had eased into a sort of comfortable routine where they spoke in generalities and reveled in each moment as it came, whether observing a stunning sunrise, working their way through a thick fog, waving to happy people on cruise ships heading north as they passed, or discussing the plans for the following day. And Conrad's humor wasn't completely absent, it just wasn't quite so raucous as before. It was always presented with an underlying hollowness as if he were keeping up appearances for Noah's sake more than his own enjoyment.

It was late one afternoon when Conrad made a suggestion that they drop anchor and take the dinghy out to one of the nearby islands for a night of camping. It would be good to stretch their legs and spend some time on land. The idea seemed inviting to Noah as well so they sailed a bit further until they came as close as they could manage to a nice stretch of beach, lowered the anchor, gathered a few supplies, and began paddling for shore.

The island did not appear very inhabited, nor did it seem unfriendly. The soft sand and sea grass were inviting and reminded Noah of his own stretch of beach in Maine in mid-

June. The two of them gathered bits of driftwood and formed a nice blazing fire just as the evening chill was setting in, then fried up some fresh fish they caught earlier that day. A small crab emerged from the sand and Conrad quickly struck it with a rock and cooked it up as an unexpected treat for them both. They finished their feast as the sun began descending before them, westward toward the channel where *The Serenade* bobbed peacefully, awaiting their return.

As they sat watching the flickering flames of their campfire, Conrad pulled out a bottle of whiskey and took several swigs before spontaneously deciding to offer it to Noah by gesturing the bottle in his direction. Noah raised his hand to refuse then thought, *What the heck?* He grabbed it from Conrad's hand, taking a swig of his own after only a slight hesitation as he took in its strong aroma. It was his first taste of alcohol and it was bitter on his tongue and burned his throat and stomach as it went down. He attempted to hide his disgust and took another sip to humor Conrad, who was laughing at the grimace he couldn't fully suppress.

"No good?" He asked heartily.

Noah swiftly gave the bottle back, "Blech, I really don't know what you see in the stuff." His eyes watered as he still couldn't shake the tarry flavor.

"You develop a taste for it." Conrad said as he took

another swig then handed the bottle back to Noah.

Despite his immediate distaste for the drink, Noah kicked the bottle back one more time before calling it quits. He supposed it was because it felt like a father-son moment that he never had with his own dad. Conrad continued drinking a bit more and the alcohol began to settle in for them both. Noah wasn't drunk, but his body was so unused to the effects of hard liquor that he did feel a bit lightheaded. Conrad was becoming inebriated himself and his lips began to loosen a bit for the first time in days.

"Do you miss her?" He asked.

Noah was taken off guard. "Huh? You mean Lily?"

Conrad nodded. "No other."

"Yes of course, terribly. I mean, this trip has been incredible, but I am looking forward to getting back home so we can begin building a life together."

"You really do love her, don't you?"

"Yes, more than anything. She's my best friend." Noah wondered at this new line of questioning.

"Well, I hope for your sake you're right about her, kid. Women have a way of pulling the rug out from under ya. Just when you give them your heart and you're ready to lay it all on the line, they smash it to pieces." In perfect timing, Conrad threw the bottle into the fire, the glass making a loud noise as it broke into a thousand shards and the residual alcohol caused the flames to shoot higher into the sky.

The action startled Noah and he jumped slightly before responding. "I don't doubt Lily's love whatsoever. She's my soulmate, if there is such a thing. I wouldn't be here right now if it wasn't for her faith in me."

Conrad had a look of dejection. "If that's true, you are one lucky man, Noah. Not too many men find a girl like that. Trust me."

Noah couldn't resist the opening. "What about you, Conrad? Have you ever had someone special like that in your life?"

Conrad stood up and looked directly into the fire instead of at Noah, "I thought I did. Once. Turned out to be nothing more than a lie." Noah stayed silent, allowing room for Conrad to continue. "She was beautiful though, my Marianne. That's her name ya know."

"What happened?" Noah whispered.

"She betrayed me, that's what. I went away for a little while and she went and married my brother. Everyone knew what a fool they made of me, even my mamma and daddy put on the wedding, and when I got home it was too late. She was already getting ready to have his baby. I'll never forget the look on her face either when I saw her the first time after I returned. I tried to scoop her up into my arms for a kiss, but she held out her hand with the ring on it. Oh, she said she was *very* sorry, but insisted she loved Frank now. My sweet baby brother, Frank. Practically raised him. He looked up to me and I taught him everything he knew about fishing and boating. Well, he went and stabbed me in the back by pursuing my girl first chance he got. Told her I was no good, that I promised all the girls I loved them and that I wasn't coming back. He knew it was a lie, but he claimed he fell so in love with Marianne that he didn't know what came over him."

"Well, I swore that day I'd never love another living soul like I loved Frank and Marianne. They begged my forgiveness, but I refused to give it. And I wasn't going to sit around and watch them build their happy little family, so I let the lot of them know I was going away forever and that's what I've done. So now you know why I have no interest in going back to Louisiana or seeing my family. I take care of myself now and no woman will ever get a chance to hurt me like that again."

Noah felt deeply sorry for his friend. Somehow he knew putting his arm around Conrad would not be warmly met and instead, he responded with empathy. "I'm sorry Conrad, I can't even imagine how much that must have hurt. But maybe one day you could try to love again. Maybe if you could find *your* soulmate. Don't give up just because one girl didn't work out."

"You don't understand how much I loved her, Noah," he replied sharply. "I would have died for this woman. I went away to make enough money to set her up for a good life and I would have given everything for her. Instead, she chose to live in poverty with my brother who barely had anything to his name. But that's how I got *The Serenade*. I took all the money I accumulated for our life together and bought that beautiful girl with it instead. *She* is my soulmate." He pointed out toward the noble schooner. "*She* has had never let me down."

It seemed sad that Conrad put all his affection into an inanimate object which could not truly love him back. Noah almost didn't dare to say the next words, but thinking back on his own experience with Lily and Everett and he and Ruth, he had to speak. "Maybe she really loved him though, Conrad. You have to accept that as a possibility. Yes, we can love people who just don't love us back, but it doesn't mean they were wrong. You wouldn't want a girl who didn't love you, would you? But I'm sure there is a girl out there that would truly love you if you'd give it half a chance."

Conrad was in no mental capacity to be reasonable. "Forget the whole thing Noah, let's just go to bed." And with that Conrad stumbled into the dark to go relieve himself, then returned, crashing on the sand and knocking out for the night. Noah knew there was nothing more that could be said.

He wasn't quite tired yet, so instead, he laid looking up at the night sky, listening to the waves crash lightly along the shore and thought of his dear Lily. He was reminded once again that not everyone was as fortunate as they were to find each other so early in life, so he vowed once again to never to take her for granted. *I wonder what she's doing tonight.* He wondered, then fell asleep to the image of her smiling face and the sound of her joyful laughter dancing across his mind.

CHAPTER SEVENTEEN

The next morning Noah had the rare privilege of waking before Conrad. There was still a bit of chill in the air, but it didn't stop him from taking a dip in the sea. He was from the Great North after all where this kind of morning was a passing luxury. The water was warm on his skin as the waves gently lapped over him. Being on the west side of the island meant the water was fairly calm.

Once he'd satisfied his desire to get a swim in, he wandered the beach gathering more driftwood to keep the fire stoked so that they could enjoy a hot breakfast. Before he reached the campsite, he could see Conrad was already up, sitting in front of what was left of the fire with his favorite worn-out flannel blanket wrapped around his shoulders. Noah dropped the driftwood directly into the makeshift fire pit and took a seat next to him.

"So, what's on the itinerary for today?" He asked, breaking the awkward silence that hung over them from the night before.

"After breakfast we'll shove off. We should reach Florida in a week's time." Conrad paused and then continued. "Hey. sorry for dumping all of that on you last night. I guess that's the price you pay when you have a little too much to drink. It doesn't take much to make a fool of yourself."

Noah was glad he brought the topic up so he wouldn't have to. "It's fine, Conrad. I totally understand. We all have our story and it's good to know a little more about yours."

"Well, there is one more thing. You know that fight I got into in Cape May? That wasn't just a friend. That was my cousin, Gus. He owed me some money from way back and we got to drinking and talking and I lost track of time. He brought up Frank and Marianne and spoke of their happiness and five kids. And he told me I should forgive them and also how my parents were worried sick about me. I told him it was none of his business and to just give me the money so I could leave. He said he wouldn't until I heard everything he had to say, so I laid him out and he got a good one in himself. I guess I lost my temper. Well, we talked a bit more after that and made things right, but I'm still hot over the whole thing. I guess after this many years I should move on, but my love for her is still like yesterday and so is my resentment toward my brother. I'm just not ready to go back and don't know if I ever will be."

Noah pitied Conrad for his broken heart, having suffered his own fears of losing Lily at one time, but knew pity was the last thing he'd want. He didn't know what words of hope to offer though. *If there's one thing I'm learning*, he thought, *the world is a big place with lots of women. But the more women I see the more I recognize what a treasure I've found.* Perhaps it wasn't so easy to find love again after all and the idea of ever losing Lily set a panic in Noah's heart as he saw himself in Conrad now. He began to understand how he came to be so wild and reckless.

The urge to head home came on very strong and Noah told himself that he would press on to his destination, but he wouldn't stay long before heading back to Boston. He knew Lily would be angry with him momentarily that he cut his trip short after all of her insisting he go, but surely her ire would quickly wane with the realization that they could be together for good.

No more was said, which seemed to suit Conrad just fine. The two of them ate a quick breakfast, packed up their belongings in the dinghy, and headed back to *The Serenade.* Once on board, they were back on track and moving quickly toward their destination. *It won't be much longer, my love*, Noah thought. *I'll be coming for you shortly!*

Mrs. Stephens had barely come to her senses the following day except to insist that Lily return to school to resume her studies. Lily was surprised, given the circumstances, as she assumed her mother would need her more than ever while her father's fate still lay undetermined. Finishing school was equally important to Lily, but her loved ones took priority over any personal ambitions she might have. Still, her mother insisted and enrolled Lily the following morning and she had no choice but to comply.

"How will you manage without me, mama?" Lily asked sincerely.

"I will do just fine, my dear girl. I appreciate you

wanting to look out for me, but I've been around many more years than you and will manage quite well. Besides, I need to check-in for any new information about your papa and see if a meeting can be arranged soon. So don't worry for my sake, I will be waiting when you get home."

Lily found her mother's cool demeanor somewhat unconvincing but gathered up her school bag and headed into the schoolhouse without further discussion. The building was much smaller than the brick institute she attended in Boston, not to mention more primitive. There was a classroom for her grade level and she entered it with much trepidation, wondering what all the strange faces would make of her. The teacher helped usher her in and gave a warm introduction. All eyes seemed to pierce through her as if they already knew the secret of what her father was being accused of, but of course, that was just Lily's imagination.

Of the fourteen students, there was only one that was familiar with the Stephens family at all. Lily's spirits lifted when she recognized the smile blazoned across the face of Ruth's beau, Wade. She was thankful that the teacher directed her to take the empty seat next to him, which she did quickly to get out from under everyone's penetrating gaze. Lily thrived in social settings but was never comfortable being the center of attention.

"Why, hello there, Miss Lily, it's great to see you," Wade formally welcomed her as she breathlessly took her seat.

"You too," she whispered back. "So nice to see a familiar face."

Wade seemed pleased to be the only one who knew the new, interesting student that all his classmates were naturally curious about. When they broke for lunch, Lily was approached by several students who greeted her enthusiastically. They asked where she was from and what brought her to Newland. Just as she was feeling a bit overwhelmed by the line of questioning, Wade came to her rescue and explained she was already a summer visitor and well acquainted with several Newland families. A couple more questions about Boston came from students who had never left their small Maine town and then Lily managed to break away for a quiet walk outside among the trees that lined the schoolyard. Wade offered to join her to "fend off any more of the press corps", to which Lily laughed softly and welcomed the company.

"So, aside from the sudden onslaught of eager classmates, how is your first day going so far?"

Lily considered the question carefully. "I really don't know, it's too early to tell. I still feel a bit out of sorts. I knew going back to school was inevitable, but it all happened so fast.

My mother rushed to enroll me this very morning. It will be a nice distraction though."

"A distraction from what, exactly?" Wade asked.

"From missing Noah, for one." She stopped short of adding the concerns for her father. "I'm mostly glad to be here though. I just need to catch up a little since the move has put me behind a bit."

"You're a bright girl, I have no doubts you'll get along just fine," Wade reassured her.

Lily smiled gratefully. "I hope to concentrate on my art a little bit as well. I'd like to impress Noah with my progress when he gets back."

"I know how you feel." Wade sighed dramatically. "I am working on a French recipe in hopes of impressing Ruth with a special dinner in the near future."

"That sounds lovely! How is Ruth since we last got together?" Lily was more than happy to take the subject off herself.

Wade brightened at Ruth's name, almost as though he were recalling a special memory. "She's doing well. She's very busy making mittens, gloves, and blankets to give the needy this winter season. She has found so much purpose in her knitting and sewing skills and has been able to help out the church with their local charities in a special way. You should see the look of joy on the faces of the recipients. Never has anyone seen such beautiful designs, or so they say. It's actually much too good for charity. She could sell them for a killing, but Ruth has no desire to make a profit from her work. Isn't that just peachy of her?"

Wade's boasting about Ruth was touching. "You must really admire all the good work she does."

"Yes, I sure do. She is an incredibly giving person." Wade beamed.

The bell suddenly rang, so the two of them headed back into the school to finish their classes for the day. What started as a day filled with anxiety now brought about a good deal of satisfaction. Lily was now pleased to be back in class, and it helped to have a friend to assist in her adjustment. She couldn't wait to get home to tell her mother all about it. If only Mrs. Stephens's day had been as promising.

CHAPTER EIGHTEEN

The walk home from school was pleasant. Lily was bundled up in her long, wool coat which made the chilly air bearable. It also helped that the sun was shining, which warmed her in spite of the early November cold. Almost all the leaves had fallen by now, though some still clung to their branches for dear life. The air carried the icy scent of winter which was a reminder of the snowy days that were close at hand, as was the partially frozen path that crunched beneath her feet.

Lily made her way along the outlet where boats would pass on their way to and from the sea. There were fewer this time of year and most commercial fishers had called it quits for the season. There were still plenty of smaller rowboats, containing one or two fishermen, that were out for a good catch late in the season, mostly for sport. It was said that fishing was in a man's blood and some went out as long as the weather permitted. These same men were the first on the water with the spring thaw. Many of the fishermen were quiet sorts who kept to themselves, but it didn't stop Lily from waving cheerfully as they passed. Every so often a particularly friendly chap would wave back or call out a "Good day, miss!" which lightened her steps as she walked.

When Lily entered the blue cottage, she expected to see her mother in the kitchen preparing dinner. Instead, it was quiet and shadowy, absent of lamplight or a fire in the hearth and her mother was nowhere to be seen. Lily called out for her and a response came from her parent's bedroom. Lily peered in to find her mother curled up on the bed, wrapped in blankets.

"How are you mama, is everything okay?" She asked softly.

"Oh honey, I'm so glad you're home. I'm fine, just not feeling well. I didn't yet make it to the jailhouse but will go tomorrow. This baby is kicking hard and I just needed to lie down for a bit. Would you very much mind making dinner tonight?"

"Don't worry mama, I'll take care of it," was Lily's assuring reply, though anyone who knew her was aware of the fact that she wasn't much of a cook. Back in Virginia and Boston her parents always had a housekeeper to help prepare meals. Mrs. Stephens knew her way around a kitchen and would cook for her family often, but never took the time to teach Lily. She never considered how important it might be someday, and it certainly was a skill that would be helpful right about now.

Lily entered the kitchen, unsure of what she should make, and pulled a few simple ingredients out of the cupboards. It took her a few moments to light the stove, but soon she had the makings of a simple stew. She planned to pair it with a buttered roll. It wasn't as easy as all that though. She overcooked the beefy chunks, leaving them tough and chewy. The broth was little more than water and a bit of light seasonings. All in all, the meal was barely edible, but her mother didn't seem to care since she had no appetite herself anyway.

Lily choked down what she could and decided that if she was to be more of a help in the kitchen during this difficult time that she would need to learn to cook. It was then that a brilliant idea came to her mind, one that would both help her mother out and would be a fun skill to surprise Noah with when he returned. She was so giddy with excitement at the plan she was formulating that even finding there was still no letter from Noah awaiting her couldn't bring her down entirely.

The next day at school Lily was eager to get a moment alone with Wade. Immediately after the bell rang to signal their lunch break, she asked him if he would stay behind for a minute.

"How may I help you, mademoiselle?" He asked, harkening back to the French accent he used the night of their dinner party with Ruth.

Lily grinned at the recollection; she was becoming quite fond of this boy. "I wondered if you might do something for me—"

"At your service." He bowed dramatically.

Lily giggled at the gesture. "Well, don't make promises you can't keep. Let me explain first." She fidgeted with a loose thread on her skirt. "You see, I wanted to ask you if you could teach me to cook. Nothing too fancy, just some basics. I'd really like to surprise Noah when he comes back and prove what a good wife I might make someday." She knew she was only telling half the truth, but it was the truth nonetheless. "And anyway, what kind of girl doesn't know how to cook? I would ask someone else, but you're the only one I know who is really any good at it. I mean, you're incredible. Who wouldn't want to learn from the best?" She flashed a toothy grin, well aware of the fact that she was abusing her charms now.

Wade chuckled at her obvious attempt to butter him up. "Alright, alright, flattery will get you everywhere. Of course I'll help you; I'd be glad to! And maybe, just maybe, we could make the arrangement mutually beneficial. How would you like to give this desperate fellow a painting lesson or two? I really need to pass my art class and so far, I'm just hopeless. I'm pretty sure our teacher has long given up on me."

"Oh my, it's a deal!" Lily exclaimed. "Though I really must warn you that I am getting the better end of the bargain."

Wade quickly chimed in. "Nonsense! I have seen your work and feel the exchange is fair indeed!"

This satisfied Lily totally. "When can we start?"

"Well, you tell me when you'd like to begin."

Lily was eager to get to work. "The sooner the better, tonight even!"

Wade was impressed by her fortitude. "I'm game, let's do it!"

So, it was settled and the plans were set for Wade to come over to Lily's house for cooking and painting lessons. She truly couldn't believe her luck! Perhaps everything would work out after all.

When Lily got home from school her mother was lying in bed once again. "What's wrong mama, not feeling well again today?"

Mrs. Stephens sighed. "Oh Lily, I just can't manage to get up right now. Would you mind making dinner again tonight? Maybe I can give you some pointers this time."

Lily brightened. "Actually mama, a friend from school named Wade is coming over to give me some cooking lessons. Do you remember I told you about him from Ruth's dinner party? He is going to be a professional chef one day. He will help me prepare a nice dinner, so you just rest."

"That sounds great dear," she responded flatly. "I

should tell you, I managed to get over to the jailhouse today. They let me see your father for a few minutes. The charges have not been officially stated but should be soon. Your father doesn't look good Lily, but you know how weak of a constitution he has. He is terribly unhappy and not eating much. I wish there was something we could do."

Lily's countenance fell at the mention of her father. "Poor papa. Isn't there some way we can help raise his spirits until he is able to come home?"

"I'm afraid not, honey. I don't know if he'll ever be happy again. And he gives me very little assurance that he will be found innocent. It looks like we may be on our own for a while."

Tears began to well up in Lily's brown eyes, "Does he still say he didn't do it?"

Mrs. Stephens was too numb to participate in Lily's emotional display, "It doesn't matter what he says, it only matters what the authorities believe and right now I don't know what's going to happen to your father. Pray for him Lily and pray for this little one on the way." Her mother rubbed her large, swollen belly. Lily knew it wouldn't be long now before she would meet her new sister or brother.

"Oh mama," she wailed. "Everything's going to be alright. I promise, somehow I'll make sure we're alright." She hugged her mother, though she didn't have the energy to embrace her back.

"Let me get some rest now honey," she said after Lily released her. "We can talk more about this tomorrow, okay? Just get dinner ready and hopefully I'll be up and feel well enough to have a little bite to eat."

Lily left the room so her mother could rest, closing the door behind her. Never had she felt so alone as she did standing in the dark, silent hallway. She shivered, though it wasn't a chill from the cold but from fear. A growing, gnawing fear that things were worse than she really understood—that life as she had always known it would never be the same again. She determined that she must push such troubling fears aside, wiped the tears from her cheeks, and decided to focus on preparing for Wade's arrival.

Within thirty minutes there was a knock at the door and Lily answered. Wade had a couple of sacks filled with seasonings and cooking utensils—just enough to get her started, he said. His cheery mood helped clear her mind of the dark thoughts that plagued her. Instead, she decided to focus on the task at hand.

They entered the kitchen together and immediately got to work. Wade showed Lily how to cut and prepare a variety of vegetables. Lily took notes in her favorite little notebook. He then showed her how to cook meat to prepare a stew—the right way. Wade complimented Lily often on how quickly she was catching on and before they both knew it, the pot of stew was simmering and filled the house with a delicious aroma.

"Wow Wade, I can't believe how much I've learned already!" Lily said in amazement as she considered what was accomplished since the time of his arrival. "Let's go try our hand at painting while the stew continues to simmer."

Lily brought out her easel and a fresh canvas, along with some paints and brushes. She walked Wade through their latest assignment by showing him some brush stroke techniques as he laid down his base for a forest with a river running through it. She explained perspective and dimension based on where objects were placed in the background and also consistency for light and shadows. After about an hour they decided to check on the stew, which appeared to be ready.

Wade took a spoon and dipped it into the broth then brought it to his lips to cool. He took a taste and added a bit more salt. He took another taste and then pinched his fingers together, brought it to his lips and kissed them away to indicate it was "perfecto." He then took a spoon to allow Lily to taste it as well. She was amazed by the improvement from the night before and what a difference could be made in the flavor of a simple stew by following Wade's easy recipe.

"Looks like dinner will be served shortly. Would you like to stay and eat?" Lily offered.

"I appreciate the invitation, but I should be running home. Good news is, we made enough to last you a couple meals. Would you like to try a new dish on Thursday? I am thinking something like a grilled fish with lemon and coleslaw."

Lily nodded. "That sounds wonderful! Same time? We can work on the next phase of your painting too."

And with plans firmly set Wade headed off for home while Lily prepared a couple of bowls with the stew and laid out the entire supper on the dining room table for two. Lily then softly knocked on her mother's door to let her know dinner was ready, but she did not receive an answer. She knocked again and no reply. She finally opened the door slowly to find her mother still fast asleep. Lily walked over and tapped her lightly on the shoulder, but her mother barely budged. It looked like Lily would be eating alone once again. The saddest part was that she had no one to show off her new cooking skills to.

CHAPTER NINETEEN

One more week at sea made all the difference. The landscape had changed dramatically over one night. For the first time ever, Noah saw palm trees with his own eyes. No longer were they just pictures in a book, a painting on a wall, or something in his dreams, but he was actually seeing them in person, and they were every bit as exotic as he imagined them to be. It made the progress of the journey that much more evident, and Noah could hardly believe he was finally on the cusp of reaching his destination after two months at sea.

The warm breeze blew all around his exposed skin.

Noah was wearing a short-sleeved button-up shirt with the top button undone. His hair had gotten longer during his time at sea and had become a tousled mess, but it felt great as the wind whipped through it. A beard covered his young face as he hadn't bothered to shave in the last couple of weeks. He knew he looked a bit of a mess, but he felt like a man just now as he stood at the ship's helm sailing alongside the Florida coast.

His protruding toothy grin was well hidden beneath the facial hair, but the one thing that had not changed was the softness in his cool blue eyes. To anyone who could discern the difference, they would have to admit they appeared wiser somehow as if years had passed, not months. Conrad once said that time at sea will age a person. In Noah's case, the lessons learned were rich and matured him considerably. He was more certain of the man he was and the man he wanted to be.

Conrad appeared older and wiser too. Though he had not completely made peace with his boyhood heartbreak, he had acknowledged the pain he still felt and his reasons for becoming unhinged at times. His time bonding with Noah had also made him more responsible, even against his will. He couldn't help it, he cared for the young man and wanted to live up to the image he had of him. He was broken and knew it would take time to forgive himself for all the damage he had done in recent years, yet, somehow he felt more whole than he had been in a long time.

Throughout the day the two men spoke eagerly of arriving at their port in the Florida Keys and what they would do as soon as they were docked and back on land. Conrad was back to his old jovial self, full of excitement and stories to tell. They had made very few stops the last couple weeks and both were itching to get out and join the living again. Noah was especially anxious to send out a letter to Lily to let her know once and for all that he arrived. In fact, he would make it his first order of business.

"Conrad," he said late in the morning, "I have to be honest with you. I've given it some thought and I don't think I'll be going back to Maine with you in the spring. It's not that I wouldn't love to stay and take in all that the south has to offer, it's just, I'm homesick for Lily. I plan to stay a short while until I hear from her and then head back by train."

Conrad kept a steady gaze to the horizon then answered. "I know. I figured you might. Life at sea isn't for everyone, Noah."

"It's not that. I've never enjoyed anything quite so much, and if it weren't for Lily, I may never go home again. It's just, I don't want to take the chance of losing her. It's not that I don't have faith our love can handle the separation. Hell, it already has, but I'm tired of putting our love to the test. Yes, as soon as I get Lily's first letter I'm heading back."

Conrad didn't know what to say. The truth was, he wished someone had told him to do the same once upon a time, but he didn't dare say it for he was actually quite forlorn at the idea of losing his sailing companion. He had always been happy as a loner but somehow got used to having a bit of company on those long days at sea. If he was honest with himself, he'd have to admit he was never really happy traveling those long nautical miles alone. It was his way of hiding from the world—of holding onto his anger and bitterness. The idea of going back without Noah now seemed daunting.

After a few more moments of contemplation, he finally responded. "I understand that's how you feel now, but just know you're always welcome to change your mind."

"I appreciate that, Conrad, truly," Noah said in all sincerity, though he didn't expect to have any second thoughts as he had been weighing the decision for a few days now. There was no reason to discuss the issue further. He had done his due diligence in showing proper respect to Conrad by not withholding the information. For now, he would focus all his attention on arriving at their final destination and how he would spend the coming weeks. If all went according to plan, he might even be home in time for Christmas!

But thoughts of Christmas were soon erased from his

mind as the white sandy beaches beckoned *The Serenade* into port. The lazy palm trees swaying in the subtropical breeze waved to greet them to a new paradise. There were scattered cabanas along the shore, hosting homes and shops of all kinds. The sea was a sparkling aquamarine that met the sky almost seamlessly if not for an array of light wispy clouds that graced the atmosphere.

As they drew closer to shore, Conrad took the wheel and eased into the marina like a pro. Despite their overeager desire to explore, they took their time carefully docking the boat and making sure it was properly secured and prepped for an extended stay. Noah wanted to jump ship immediately but first went down to his cabin and took a few minutes to pen his letter to Lily.

My Dearest Lily,

How I have missed you more than words can express! I have finally arrived in Florida and have attached the address of the post office where I can be reached. Please tell me quickly how you have been since we last met in Boston. I hated to leave you that day, but after having come this long distance I am certain it was the correct decision. You were right, this was a chance of a lifetime. But my greatest adventure is yet to come when you and I finally start our lives together. Not being able to maintain contact has been agony, but the only contentment I have found in our separation was believing you have thought of me every day since my departure as I have thought of you. Please write as soon as time allows and let me know if you received my little gift a month back. I know you would probably prefer a longer letter, but I have only just arrived moments ago and thought of nothing else but writing you first. So please, forgive me for being brief. Another letter will soon follow giving more details of my travels and my experiences here in Florida. Until then, I eagerly await your reply. Give my love to Aunt Prissy, I'm sure she worries about me too.

Yours Always,
Noah Sullivan

Noah quickly folded the letter and placed it securely in an envelope then resurfaced to the deck to find Conrad waiting impatiently for him to return.

"What took you so long, kid? Let's get going!"

"I had to write this letter quickly," he replied, waving it in the air before stuffing it into his pocket. "I'd like to mail it immediately, if possible. Is the post office nearby?

Conrad sighed in mock exasperation, "Yes, yes, it isn't a far walk. Let's get going lover boy. There are a few places I want to introduce you to."

Noah followed quickly behind, still in shock that he had finally made it. He followed his dream and could now rightly claim the journey a success!

CHAPTER TWENTY

It had been over a week since Lily and Wade started tutoring each other and so far they were both progressing nicely. Wade admitted that Lily was much more proficient at cooking than he would ever be at painting, but they had fun nonetheless and Wade was confident he would have no trouble getting a passing grade on his assignment after all.

Lily couldn't believe how sincerely she enjoyed cooking. It was never something that much appealed to her but learning from Wade had changed her mind entirely and now she was developing a love for it. Even her mother was impressed with her rapidly progressing skills—when she would actually eat that is.

Mrs. Stephens was still struggling considerably with the pregnancy and spent most evenings in her room sleeping. Lily had not yet had a chance to visit her father and was becoming restless to do so. She missed him a great deal, especially their evening talks. Lily and her father always had such a special relationship. He was a kind, gentle soul who always offered a listening ear. Sometimes they would even spend time in the garden together, tending to the plants and talking about their day. He was the one she always counted on to give her a word of advice or believe in her, even more than her mother. Now he was gone when she needed him most.

It was certainly no secret to Lily that her father was unhappy in Boston, but she still couldn't wrap her mind around the possibility that he had done this thing of stealing from his company. It seemed so unlike her father in many ways, but even if it were true, Lily couldn't turn her back on him. Even though her mother was hesitant to take her, Lily also knew her father needed her more than ever. She wanted to obey her mother's wishes, but now determined to insist that she be allowed to visit the jailhouse to speak to her father in the next couple of days. He would have the answers to all her questions, he would tell her what she should do.

Lily had just finished preparing a small chicken and placed it in the oven when she went to check on her mother in hopes of having this discussion with her. The door to the bedroom was slightly open so she didn't even bother to knock.

"Mama?" she called softly. "Are you awake?"

Her mother turned to face her, though her eyes were barely open. "What is it, my dear?"

"I'm sorry to wake you, but it's just that…well, I want to see papa. Soon."

Lily's mother inhaled deeply. "I know you do honey, I'm sorry, I promise we'll go sometime next week."

"No mama, please," she pressed in a manner that was out of character. "I need you to take me in a day or two. I really need to speak to Papa and I know he would want to talk to me."

Lily's mother was now a little more awake and decided to sit up. "Lily, the truth is, your father loves you, but he doesn't want you to see him like this. Do you really think it's a good idea to put him in that position? Think of how hard it will be on him."

Lily didn't believe her words. "Of course I want to see him. Who cares if he's embarrassed? He's my father and we need to get through this together as a family!"

Lily's mother frowned. "I understand why you feel that

way, I just don't want to see you disappointed if your father isn't behaving like himself. It's a rough time on all of us…" Her words were suddenly cut short with a sudden cry of agony.

Lily was startled by her sudden outburst of pain and ran to her mother's side. "Are you okay mama?" She called out.

Mrs. Stephens gripped her belly and winced in pain. "I'm not sure. I think it's passing."

Lily's heart began to beat faster as she realized what was causing the pain. "Is it the baby? Do you need a doctor?" Her mother was about to answer when she screamed in pain again. Lily stood staring, waiting for a reply.

Her mother said nothing but tried to get up out of the bed and stand on her two feet. She stood still, waiting for the next wave of pain that didn't seem to come. "I think I'm okay," she said finally but she only took a couple steps when a great splash of water hit the floor. Mrs. Stephens's eyes widened and met Lily's whose were equally as large. Her mother looked down and they both knew this baby was coming.

"It's too early, isn't it mama?" Lily could feel the panic rising in her throat as she spoke.

"Only a little. It's going to be okay." She said reassuringly, trying to keep Lily calm. "Go get Mrs. Durgin and if she can head over, then go straight to the doctor and bring him quickly…go now!"

Lily did as her mother said, nearly forgetting to put on her shoes and coat. She opened the door and felt a frigid blast of cool air to remind her of her blunder. She bundled up as quickly as she could then flew out the door and into the woods toward the Durgin's house. Thankfully Mrs. Durgin was home and promised to rush over immediately. Flora was home too and asked how she could help. "Please, go with your mother in case she needs you," Lily replied.

After Mrs. Durgin and Flora were on their way, Lily sprinted back into the darkness, toward town to Dr. Fitzgerald's house. She arrived in record time and banged on the door without a moment of hesitation. A housemaid answered, somewhat perturbed by the fevered knocking.

"Please Miss, is Dr. Fitzgerald available?" Lily was still panting to catch her breath.

The housemaid did not seem affected in the least by the panic in Lily's voice, clearly accustomed to these types of pressing matters. "I'm sorry, Dr. Fitzgerald and the Missus are out for the evening. May I tell them who called?"

Lily's mind raced with what to do next. "Do you know when they'll be back? My mother is having a baby. Please tell them when they return to go to the Blue Cottage next to Birchwood Cottage. They will know the place."

The housemaid replied without any sense of urgency

to Lily's state. "Well, I'm not sure when they'll be back but I'll be sure to give them your message when they do."

She then closed the door before Lily could say anything further and she was left dumbfounded as to what she should do next. *Reverend Thomas!* Of course. It was the obvious choice as she recalled Mrs. Thomas had assisted many in the congregation who gave birth. She ran quickly to the Thomas's house and found everyone home, warming by the fire. She explained that her mother had gone into labor and the entire Thomas family wasted no time in gathering up a few things and followed Lily home.

Once there, Lily entered the home to find her mother was back in bed, laying on her back and gripping Flora's hand while Mrs. Durgin tended to her as best she could. Mrs. Thomas quickly jumped in to help, barking orders for hot water and a towel. Lily suddenly felt Reverend Thomas's hand on her shoulders as he ushered her back out into the hall.

"All will be well, Lily. Let Mrs. Thomas and Mrs. Durgin help your mother and you wait out here with me," he said kindly. "You too, Flora." He waved to Flora to join them. The door closed and the wait began.

It seemed like a lifetime before anyone emerged from the room. Every so often Lily would hear her mother scream in agony and she shook with fear. Reverend Thomas would reassure her that all was well, but Lily had never experienced anyone giving birth and the sound was quite fearsome and difficult to brush off.

Reverend Thomas finally directed her to wait in the kitchen to minimize the noise while he checked on the ladies. Ruth was there too, but she had not said a word. She had been standing quietly, ready to be of service if necessary. Lily just noticed her for the first time and apologized for not saying hello sooner.

"It's quite alright," Ruth said. "You seem worried, but Father is right, it's going to be fine." She sat down beside her and patted her hand reassuringly.

They said very little else to each other, but sat somberly at the little kitchen table when Ruth, who was looking around the room to distract herself, caught sight of something familiar.

"Isn't that Wade's cookbook?" She asked curiously.

Lily, who was in a daze, was startled by the unexpected inquiry and took a moment to process the question. "Huh? Oh, yeah. He must have left it when he was here last night."

Ruth's face went white. "Wade was here?"

Lily didn't yet see her expression and answered matter-of-factly, "Oh yes, for our cooking lessons. He must have just forgotten it."

"What do you mean, *cooking lessons*?"

Lily now realized she had said something to upset Ruth and struggled to find her words. "Oh, it's nothing. He was just helping me prepare some meals to help mama out. That's all."

Ruth was silent but Lily knew Wade must not have told her about their arrangement and she didn't know what to say at this point to avoid raising more suspicion. She was still searching for the words when Reverend Thomas re-entered.

"Lily, good news, your mama is doing well and should be ready to see you soon. I believe you have a baby brother who wants to meet you."

Lily breathed a huge sigh of relief at the good news and quickly forgot about her conversation with Ruth. She was smiling from too much joy. "A baby brother, my goodness, what a blessing!" She exclaimed.

CHAPTER TWENTY-ONE

Salty Joe's was a little bar and eatery that Noah and Conrad began to frequent since landing in Key West. It was nothing more than a tiki hut and aside from the kitchen, contained no walls or windows so that the balmy ocean breezes wafted through without obstruction. Noah was becoming familiar enough with it that he would often sit alone and kick back a beer and a bite to eat. He wasn't sure he even liked the taste of beer, but it seemed the thing to do.

On this particular evening, he took a seat at the bar, hoping to grab a quick bite then head back to the boat for an evening of reading. He thought he might try writing Lily again too. It had been two weeks since he sent his letter and still no reply. Every day he went to the post office, his heart full of hope at hearing from his beloved, and every day he went away, crestfallen at not receiving a single word.

He was puzzling over this lack of communication when one of the regular waitresses, Sylvia, approached to take his order. She was an exotic beauty with long dark tresses and flashy eyes. She was generally known for her sass and ability to shut down frisky customers, but tonight she approached Noah with a smile to indicate she wouldn't bite.

"Hello young Noah," she purred in her light accent. "All alone tonight?"

Noah nodded. "Looks like it. Conrad was out all day doing some trading and then had plans with some friends for dinner. He'll be back tomorrow, I'm sure."

Naturally, Noah assumed she was asking for Conrad as the two seemed to know each other from previous visits and their playful banter indicated a mutual attraction. For that reason, he thought nothing of it at all when she looked around then took a seat beside him.

"You look like you could use some company," she continued. "Is everything alright? You look a little sad."

Noah sighed. "Yes, I'm fine. I guess I'm just feeling a little homesick."

Sylvia gave Noah an empathetic smile. "I'm sorry to hear that, Noah. Do you not enjoy being in this beautiful place?" Sylvia placed her perfectly manicured hand on his shoulder.

"Of course I enjoy it…who wouldn't? I suppose you could say it's the people back home I actually miss."

Sylvia drew closer now. "Oh, do you have a sweetheart back home?" Her tone was one of pity.

"You could say that. Only…" He hesitated to continue. Saying it out loud would only make his frustrations a reality.

"Only, what?" Sylvia urged. She had a way of getting men to talk.

Noah was oblivious to Sylvia's charms, but in the end, couldn't resist the opportunity to vent his frustrations. "It's just that I haven't heard from her since I sent my letter out a couple of weeks ago. I'm sure her reply is just delayed in getting here, but I was hoping to make arrangements soon."

"Arrangements? What kind of arrangements?" Sylvia's hand was now on Noah's knee.

"Well, I was thinking about heading back early. To see if I could be home by Christmas, but if I wait much longer, I probably won't be able to go until after the New Year. I'm just not sure what to do next."

"Where is home, if you don't mind me asking?" Sylvia scooted in a bit more, closing the distance between her and Noah altogether.

She was now close enough that Noah could tell she smelled of coconut. He suddenly felt uncomfortable with her close-proximity and shifted in his seat to create some space between them. "Maine. But my sweetheart, for lack of a better term, is in Boston at the moment, so that is where I must go first."

Sylvia feigned shock at such a notion. "Why on earth would anyone want to go somewhere so incredibly drab this time of year when you can be in this incredible paradise with beaches and palm trees...and warm nights?" She added, her words dripping like honey in his ear as she inched nearer than even before. "If this sweetheart of yours doesn't write you then why not enjoy your time away? Maybe it would help to have a little fun. I can be sweet too, ya know?"

Amidst his growing discomfort, Noah forgot his hunger and suddenly had the urge to get started on his letter to Lily. *I think I'll write Aunt Prissy too,* he decided, hoping that he could get word from her at the very least. Noah quickly thanked Sylvia for trying to cheer him up and briefly explained that he had something he forgot to do.

He got up to leave and she gave him a little pout. "Oh

Noah, I really do like you very much. I hope you'll come back and see me. I promise to make it worth your while." She winked.

Noah didn't know how to respond to such a proposition, so he simply walked toward the exit and left. Deep down he wanted to run but knew he'd look like a fool. Instead, he merely walked with a quick step back to *The Serenade*, half hoping to find Conrad there beginning to doze off on deck as he often did. Then he wouldn't feel so lonely. Sadly, the boat was empty and Noah now found himself alone *and* hungry. He decided to make the most of the variety of snacks he stashed away in his cabin and just eat a big breakfast in the morning. After finishing off some dry crackers, Noah sat down on his favorite spot at the bow and began to write.

My Dearest Lily

I trust you have received my letters by now letting you know I arrived in Florida safely. I am a little concerned that I have not yet heard back from you to confirm this fact, but I expect there is an explanation for this, such as the mail has been delayed. The truth is, I miss you more than I can ever express. My heart aches with thoughts of only you and I long to be with you again. So much so that I'm hoping you will consider it a pleasant surprise to hear that I am planning on coming home early. I know if you were here you would insist I finish my trip, but I have made up my mind and it's settled. Please don't concern yourself that I will have regrets, I feel satisfied that I have done the thing I most wanted to do and am ready to be by your side at the first word I receive.

As for Florida, it is a beautiful change of pace from Maine, but nowhere near as close to my heart. I know you would love to see the beaches here. The seashells are enormous and in the morning I often sit on the shore and picture you walking along the sand, collecting the most beautiful ones for your collection. It feels as real to me as if you were actually there, and yet I cannot speak to you or hold you close. I hope one day to bring you to this place and show you all I've seen, but for now, I dream of snow because that is where you are. What joy is there to be found in being anywhere without you? If you were in the desert with no oasis in view, that is where I'd long to be too. Please write soon.

Yours Always,

Noah

After he set his pen down, realizing his words would seem incredibly sappy to someone like Conrad but he hoped Lily would appreciate his honesty. Noah then carefully folded the letter and put it into an envelope marked for Lily's brownstone in Boston. After taking a moment to collect his thoughts, Noah took up the pen again and began to write a letter of a different tone.

Dear Aunt Prissy,

Hello from the sunny Florida coast! I trust you and Buck are doing well. Please tell me all about your time enjoying marital bliss. Are you very much enjoying your new home? I do hope so. Have you stopped by Birchwood Cottage lately? If so, how is she holding up? Missing her master, I hope. Tell her it won't be long before I'll darken her doorstep once more.

I've been here a couple of weeks now and wanted to fill you in on all that I have seen and done, but that will have to wait for another time. I am writing in part to also inquire as to whether you or anyone in Newland has heard from Lily as of late. I wrote her the first day of my arrival and twice since and have no gotten word back that she has received any of my letters. Naturally, I am concerned.

I wondered if you might try reaching her to find out if there is any news that might put my mind at ease? I would truly appreciate it, my dear aunt. I miss you so much and can't wait to see you again soon. Give everyone my love!

Yours Truly,
Noah

Noah felt satisfied he had done his best to express his concerns and planned to drop the letters off first thing in the morning. He was confident he would hear something back soon, one way or another, and with that task put to rest, he decided to lay his head down for the night. Conrad had not returned, but Noah had worried plenty enough for the time being. It would soon be a new day and it wouldn't be long before he would get word about Lily, maybe even as early as tomorrow he would still receive a letter. And perhaps he would find he had nothing to be concerned about at all.

CHAPTER TWENTY-TWO

Lily sat contentedly on the rocker in the corner of her parent's bedroom, holding her baby brother close to her breast and rocking him back and forth. Her mother had given birth a little over two weeks ago and slowly they were beginning to settle into a new routine. Lily knew very little about babies but was learning quickly. Her mother still seemed to be struggling to help out around the house or even spend much time with the baby aside from regular feedings, so Lily assisted her as much as possible while her mother recovered.

Mrs. Thomas had not only been a godsend in helping

to deliver little Danny, whose full name was Daniel Elijah Stephens, but she also offered a great amount of assistance in providing blankets, clothing, and toys. Sometimes she and Leah would come over during the day to assist in caring for Danny so Lily could return to school, though she noticed Ruth never joined them.

Upon her return to school the following week, Lily couldn't help but observe a change in Wade's behavior toward her. Usually friendly and open, he now seemed to keep his distance and Lily began to wonder if she had said or done something to offend him. Even when she returned his favorite cookbook she got nothing more than a polite "thank you", and no offer to come over again soon to continue their lessons. Nor did he ask for additional help with his painting for art class. After two days of strictly cordial interactions, Lily decided to approach Wade and find out what the problem was, if any.

During their lunch break, she found the perfect opportunity. Wade had snuck outside for a bit of fresh air and Lily followed close behind. Once outside she called his name and he turned around to face her, realizing he had nowhere to go to avoid the discussion that was sure to follow.

"Hi Wade, how are you doing?" She asked, unsure of how to begin.

"Fine." He looked down and shuffled his feet, averting

her penetrating gaze.

Lily decided the direct approach might be best. "What's wrong? Please forgive me if I'm off base here, but are you mad at me or something?"

The jig was up. "No Lily, you have done nothing wrong," Wade admitted.

Lily was deeply puzzled. "Then what's going on? Why are you suddenly giving me the silent treatment? I thought we were friends."

"We are! I mean, we were…" He stammered.

"Were?"

Wade put his hand on his forehead in frustration. "Look you didn't do anything wrong. It's me. I messed up, okay? The day your mother went into labor, Ruth said you mentioned our cooking lessons. The problem is, I didn't tell her. So you see, this is all my fault."

This brought no great comfort to Lily. "You didn't tell her? Why?"

"You might not believe this, but I was hoping to surprise her with the painting. You see, she always speaks so highly of Noah's skills and I couldn't paint a lick. And even though I knew my artwork would never compare to his, I thought maybe it would impress her enough if I learned a bit and she'd stop swooning. After the assignment was graded I planned to give it to her as a gift. As you can imagine things didn't go over very well when I tried to explain."

Lily closed her eyes and shook her head, uncertain of how to proceed. "So now what?"

"Well, this is the hard part. She wouldn't want you to know this, but Ruth is very envious of you. Not only because of how things turned out with Noah, but she feels worried that I too might be falling in love with you. Of course, I told her that's not true. Lily, I like you a great deal, but I am in love with Ruth, truly. She wouldn't accept my reasons though."

Lily believed what he said to be true. She had seen the way Wade looked at Ruth, but now the two of them had created a real dilemma. The last thing Lily had intended to do was to hurt Ruth, but she understood why it would be taken the wrong way.

"Listen, Wade, I understand. I don't want to do anything to further aggravate the situation for you. Perhaps it truly is best if we lay low for a while, at least until Noah gets back. Once Ruth gets the reassurance she needs I am certain this will all blow over."

Wade nodded. "Yes, that might be best. Thank you for understanding. I truly am sorry for all of this, Lily. I hope you will forgive me."

Lily smiled. Wade was not the kind of person anyone

could stay mad at. "Of course I do, besides, I think I've learned enough from our lessons to make at least three good meals. What more do I need to know?" They both laughed in spite of the seriousness of the situation.

"And I've learned enough to paint at least as well as Rembrandt." He bowed playfully. "Oh, the tragedy of it all." Lily was able to manage a light chuckle at Wade's gesture and that was all the reassurance he needed to know he was forgiven. "I tell ya what," he continued, pulling the cookbook back out of his bag. "Why don't you keep this a while longer to help you with your meals. It's something anyway."

Lily was touched and took the book, "Thank you Wade, are you sure?" He nodded. "That is very kind! I promise to take good care of it and will give it back as soon as I feel a little more confident with my skills. I wish I could return the favor somehow. What about your art class?"

"I think I've peaked," Wade replied, flashing Lily a toothy grin.

It seemed there was nothing more to say, so with that they headed back in, both feeling relieved, if not a bit sad that their friendship was being cut short. Lily had begun relying on that friendship to help her get through the school year, but it looked like she was on her own once again. *Well, I guess that gives me more incentive to study*, she thought.

While it was easy to feel forlorn over this disappointing development, Lily went home that afternoon with something heavier on her mind than the situation with Wade and Ruth. She still hadn't seen her father and recently it was revealed that charges were officially being made against him and he would likely stand trial for embezzlement of company funds. This weighed heavily on both her and her mother and only made matters worse at home. Lily knew it was time to make that visit and speak to her father face to face, with or without her mother's consent. She decided the only thing to do was leave for school the next morning but go down to the jailhouse instead.

Early the next morning she got up to ready herself and did all she could to talk herself up into going through with her plan. She really hated to go behind her mother's back but any time she raised the issue her mother kept putting their visit off for another time. If it wasn't the baby being born, it was the extra stress it would put on her father, or the visiting hours had changed. This time nothing would stop Lily from seeing him.

Mrs. Thomas stopped by bright and early with Leah at her side. Leah gave Lily a shy smile and waved, a huge gesture for the girl, and Lily gave her a slice of the apple pie she baked the night before. Leah seemed content as she sat in the kitchen, savoring each bite. Meanwhile, Mrs. Thomas spoke to Lily.

"If I'm being completely honest, I am worried about your mama, Lily." She said in a serious tone. "It is not like a woman to be so detached from their newborn. I know the doctor says she is suffering from exhaustion, but you may have noticed she's even having a hard time feeding him on schedule these past couple days."

Certainly Lily had noticed her mother was not acting like herself but blamed it on the stress of the situation. "Mama just needs time is all. The past few months have been hard on all of us. Please be patient with us Mrs. Thomas, I promise to do all I can to help."

Mrs. Thomas placed a reassuring hand over Lily's, "It's not that dear girl, I will be here for you as much as I can, it's just that I do have many duties at the church that I have been neglecting and well, it's all fine and good that you are taking up so much of the slack yourself, but a baby needs his mother."

Lily was now certain she needed her father's wisdom. "Yes, Mrs. Thomas, I understand. I will do all I can to encourage her. Thank you for your concern and all you have done. I really don't want to keep you from your duties. If necessary, I will drop out of my classes until Noah comes back."

Mrs. Thomas now appeared a tad flush. "Oh, that isn't

necessary child. We will find a way to make it work. I'm just worried is all. Mr. Thomas tells me I do far too much worrying for a woman my age. I suppose I get it from my own mother. Anyway, off you go. A girl should be learning while she still can. God knows that there is little time in life for education once you start having little ones of your own."

Lily somehow suspected she was speaking of herself. The truth was, Mrs. Thomas was a bright woman but spent most of her time running around town delivering baskets and clothing to the needy and when she was home she tended to her husband and children. Leah was a handful in her own right, as she demanded certain routines just to function and no one understood why she was that way. Lily imagined in another lifetime that Mrs. Thomas might have been a teacher or could even have worked for some political cause, but despite her inner-groanings, she seemed content being a pillar of the community. If nothing else, she had everyone's respect and admiration.

Mrs. Thomas then proceeded to push Lily out the door and promised everything would be taken care of until she returned. Lily was relieved to leave the house but was now anxious to get to the task at hand as she saw the necessity of it more than ever. She knew what she had to do and began marching toward town with much determination. Today she would finally speak to her poor father, face to face. Hopefully, he could help her make sense of everything once and for all.

CHAPTER TWENTY-THREE

As Lily approached the jailhouse her nerves began to kick in. The walk over had been one so driven by her conviction that she should see her father that she was taken off guard by the sudden intimidation she felt once she found herself staring up at the cold, imposing building of the jailhouse. She swallowed hard then began her ascent up the steps that led to the entrance.

Once inside she walked straight toward the receptionist who sat at a long desk littered with paperwork. The woman's hair was pulled back into a tight bun and she wore reading glasses set at the tip of her nose, causing her to look down at Lily as she approached. The rest of the room was plain with no artwork on the walls, only various certificates and legal announcements.

“Hello young lady, is there something I can help you with?” The woman inquired, preempting Lily’s approach.

Lily flashed a smile to hide the uncertainty creeping up inside her. “Yes, I am here to see Peter Stephens.”

The lady was all business. “And what may I ask is your relation to the inmate?”

Lily had not thought of her father as an inmate and it made her blush suddenly. “I am his daughter," she said timidly, feeling ashamed.

The woman smiled compassionately at Lily’s reply and she asked her to wait a moment so she could check with her superior about allowing her to enter. She motioned for Lily to have a seat in one of the stiff wooden chairs lined up along the adjacent wall, then excused herself and disappeared through a door behind her that seemed to lead to a dark hallway.

Fifteen minutes later she returned with an officer who motioned her to accompany him through the door, into that dark hallway and into the holding cell. There were four cells in all, two of which were empty and one that held a man with a long, grey beard sleeping on a cot with a thin blanket draped over his bony shoulders. Not exactly the looks of a hardened criminal, but this was Newland after all.

The fourth was of course occupied by her father, who was standing inside the jail cell, his hands wrapped tightly around the bars in anticipation of his daughter's arrival.

"Papa!" Lily cried out and rushed to place her hands over his. In just a few short weeks her father looked like a shell of the man she knew. He had lost a considerable amount of weight and dark circles had formed under his eyes. Eyes that once sparkled with life were now dark and sad. The only light that escaped them now was the small joy of seeing his daughter.

"Lily," he spoke in return. "It's so good to see you. But what are you doing here? Did your mother bring you?" He looked over her shoulder to see if his wife was also there.

"No papa, mama doesn't know I'm here. I came by myself because I had to see you. To make sure you are okay."

Tears filled her father's eyes as he looked at the concern on Lily's face. She was sure they were tears of joy for her act of love, but they were something else entirely. "Sweetheart, you really shouldn't have come. This is no place for a little girl."

Lily's heart cracked. "I'm not a little girl papa, so you don't need to protect me. I am your daughter and it was important to me that I see you."

Her father hung his head in shame at his daughter's tender words and became angry that she put him in this position. "Dammit Lily, did it ever occur to you that I asked your mama not to bring you here? That maybe I don't want you to see me like this? You should be in school right now, focusing on your studies and being with friends."

Lily was taken back by her father's harsh tone. "I don't understand you, Papa. How could you think I wouldn't want to see you after everything that's happened? Besides, I may not have any studies to worry about soon. I'm thinking about leaving school to help Mama. She's not doing very well you know. And now the baby..."

"What about the baby?" Lily's father turned somber.

"Don't you know? Mama had the baby two weeks ago. It's been a hard time for her."

The news did not illicit an immediate reply and the moment of silence between them made the room feel like a tomb. "No, I didn't know," he said finally. "Your mama hasn't been to see me in a while. I figured she needed a break from all this. Please, tell me. What is the baby like?"

Lily was now sorry that she had been so curt in how she delivered the news. She softened at the sight of pain on her father's face. "It's a boy papa, his name is Daniel. We've been calling him Danny."

Her father smiled at the news. "Daniel. I've always liked that name. My favorite character in the Bible. Your grandmother used to read me the story often when I was a little boy. Funny to think that back then that lions were my greatest fear. Didn't like to stand too close to their cage at the zoo. Now look at me. On the other side of the cage. I am the lion. I am seen as the dangerous one."

Lily didn't want to interrupt her father, but she was confused as to why he would compare himself to a lion. The puzzled look on her face said enough.

"Lily, I'm sorry to tell you this," he continued. "I wish I could protect you from all the problems I have caused you and your mama, but the truth is, I am probably going to prison for a while."

Lily drew closer and grabbed her father's hands through the cell bars. "So, you did it then? It's true?" He couldn't say the words out loud, but his silence told Lily everything she needed to know. "How could you, Papa? Why?" She begged.

"I guess I was sick of working hard all my life and having nothing to show for it. It seemed like no matter what I did we could never get ahead. And now in Boston, putting in so many hours. Working to please my boss and seeing him pat this one on the back and promote this one while I was overlooked. It didn't matter how good I was at my job; I was never part of the good ol' boys club. What can I say? I was bitter and angry and wanted to prove I was smarter than all of them."

"But you had us, papa, wasn't that enough?" Lily began to cry.

"I know it should have been, but I suppose I saw an opportunity to even the score and I took it. Once I started tampering with the accounts I couldn't stop. It was so easy, and it was the reason we were able to live comfortably in such a nice home. Your mama was finally happy to have nice things and no one suspected a thing. By the time I realized what I'd done I didn't know how to get out of it. I tried to stop, but it all just got out of control and I knew I'd never have enough money to pay it all back. A few months went by and I thought maybe no one would ever notice, but some of the managers began looking into the records and could see things weren't adding up. The walls were closing in and the only thing I knew to do was leave town and hope they'd never trace it back to me."

Lily's tears flowed hot and fast now. The man she had looked up to her whole life, who she always admired for his work ethic and honesty, who had loved her so well when she needed his assurance, had now revealed his true character. He was weak and foolish. But Lily loved him anyway. He was still her father, but she needed time to process all she had learned.

"Thank you, Papa," she said sincerely. "I'm glad to finally know the truth once and for all…and to hear it from you. I wish I knew what to say, but I need some time to think. Perhaps I better go now, but I will try to see you again soon," she added.

But her father could not ask her to return. Instead, he kissed her hands and told her good-bye. "Please don't tell your mother you came to see me," was his final request which Lily agreed would be best to honor under the circumstance. She knew the truth now and that was all that mattered.

Lily left the jailhouse and was hit by a biting cold wind that stung her face from the wet tears that had yet to dry. Light flakes were falling and dusted the steps and pathway leading her away from the man who was once her hero but proved to be nothing but mere flesh. The future suddenly looked dark and hopeless.

The next day Lily got word, along with the rest of Newland, that her father had been formally changed and would be going to court for sentencing soon. He was going to plead guilty so the case would probably be settled quickly. With any luck, people would soon forget and move onto other topics of interest. Lily knew in her heart that life would never be simple again though. That there were difficult challenges ahead.

Her mother had little reaction to the news. She spent most of the day in bed and wandered around the house in a state of complacency, barely acknowledging Lily or tending to Danny. When she did speak, she was mostly irritable, not wanting to be bothered even to eat. So much now rested on Lily's shoulders.

Lily's concern for her mother was growing over the days and weeks. She felt powerless to fix the situation and only knew to help where her mother was failing. She wanted to rise to the occasion, but the pressure was becoming too much for a young girl to bear alone. There was now no question in her mind, she was ready to ask Noah to come home. She didn't want it to come to this, but she truly needed him. The only problem was, why hadn't he written? He should have arrived in Florida by now.

CHAPTER TWENTY-FOUR

Lily awoke to a pounding on the front door. Her mother was still sleeping, as was little Danny. In an effort to keep them from waking, she quickly threw on her robe and ran to answer it. Standing in three inches of snow was Flora, pink and smiling brightly from the news she brought.

"Lily, I'm so glad you're awake, you won't believe it!" She said breathlessly.

Lily's mind quickly ran through the possibilities of what Flora could be referring to. Did she have word about Noah? Her father? "What is it my dear girl?" She urged.

"It's Everett! He's back. He came in last night."

Lily hadn't heard from Everett in some time, and he had not really crossed her mind, but suddenly she understood the good news. "Really?" She exclaimed. "What on earth brought him back to Newland? Everything is okay, I hope?"

Flora's grin widened further, "Oh yes, everything is fine. I wrote him last week and told him all that was going on and he said he planned to come home first thing to make sure all was well."

Lily blushed deeply now. "Oh Flora, he shouldn't have done that. What did you say to make him think he had to pick up and move back so suddenly?"

"Oh Lily, don't concern yourself with such nonsense. You should know by now; I tell my brother everything. Of course, you shouldn't be surprised that he would be concerned, especially since you haven't heard from Noah since you left Boston and…"

"You told him that?" Lily interrupted, her voice rising from embarrassment.

"Well yeah, we're all concerned for you Lily. I'm sure Noah has a perfectly good explanation, but with your dad gone and all, we just want to help in whatever way we can. Plus, Everett has been terribly homesick. Don't be mad at me, please. You are like family to us."

It was difficult for Lily not to feel humiliated under the circumstance, but the joy of seeing Everett overrode her desire to be cross with Flora. "When can I see him?" she asked.

"He's still sleeping after his long trip, but I suspect he'll be by this afternoon. Anyway, I just wanted to give you a heads up. Oh, Lily, we're so glad he's home and I know everything is going to be just fine!"

Lily hugged Flora tightly then sent her on her way. Lily knew it wasn't Everett's job to take care of her or her family, but hope welled up within her at the thought of seeing her good friend again and knowing she would have additional support during this difficult time.

She spent the rest of the morning getting the house ready for visitors. Mrs. Stephens was slow to get around but by late morning she was properly dressed and sitting in her father's chair, holding the baby and watching indifferently while Lily ran to-and-fro throughout the house finishing up last minute tasks and preparing a light lunch, should their guests be hungry.

Shortly after noon, she heard the Durgin's approach the blue cottage. Flora was being particularly talkative, which gave them away. Anxious, Lily ran to open the door before they even had a chance to knock. "Hello, please come in!" She called out.

"Not before getting a hug," Everett said as he approached her, wrapping his strong arms around her waist and lifting her effortlessly off the ground. Lily hugged Everett back tightly, happy to see her dear friend once again.

"My goodness Everett, it feels like it's been so long, how have you been?" She got a look at his face now. She recognized the boy she knew, but he was older now, both in appearance and in his countenance. His eyes looked world-weary, though his lopsided grin had not changed. His hair was shorter and no longer fell over his brow. She wondered in what ways she appeared different to him as well.

"Well, it was a long trip, but a bit of rest will do a soul good! It's great to be back, Lily."

Everyone entered and took a seat in the main living space. Her mother barely even managed a polite hello, which was so unlike her usual hospitable self. Flora was giddy with excitement at having her beloved brother home which eliminated any awkwardness that might have been otherwise evident. "Everett says he'll stay as long as he needs to. I hope he never goes back to that stinky ol' Portland again. Newland is so much more pleasant, plus me and Lily are here."

Everett blushed at the implication of his sister's words. Lily decided to save him by offering them tea or a bite to eat. They all moved to the dining room upon accepting her gracious offer of soup and sandwiches with tea, which made for a lovely afternoon of catching up.

"So, Everett, Flora tells me you were slated for a promotion in Portland. Are you sure you want to give that up?" Lily asked with genuine curiosity.

"Oh, there are more important things to life than money and the shipyards will always be there if I need work. I'm actually really glad to be home. I plan to go over to the market first thing in the morning and see about getting my old job back. At least to begin with. I am sure there are plenty of opportunities here to hold me over."

His answer satisfied Lily for the time being, but she couldn't help feeling guilty just the same. It seemed an awfully big sacrifice to make on her account, but she appreciated his willingness to be there for her and seeing Everett now reminded her how much she truly missed him.

"Well, to echo what our dear Flora has repeated several times this afternoon, your return home is a joyful occasion for us all." Everett smiled warmly in response to that sentiment.

The following day was Sunday and Lily was pleased that Everett decided to join her and the rest of the Durgin family at church. Her mother was not feeling well and couldn't make it, so instead, she accompanied the Durgin's over to the chapel by herself. She missed the days when she and her parents would attend together, so it was nice to not feel she was going alone.

When they entered the small chapel, they were immediately spotted by the parishioners who had already arrived. Several came over to find out to what they owed the honor of Everett's sudden appearance, while others patted him on the back to simply welcome him home. Ruth and Wade were among the crowd, Wade treading very carefully in Lily's presence.

Reverend Thomas had also come over to greet the young man, and Mrs. Thomas, who was speaking to an elderly lady, finally wandered over as well. Leah stayed in her usual seat, unaware of the commotion.

"It sure is good to see you again, son," The Reverend stated. "How long do you plan to stay?"

"No plans to head back any time soon. I suppose you could say I was missing my loved ones."

The answer satisfied Reverend Thomas and Lily was relieved that Everett hadn't made a spectacle of her situation by admitting the real reason for his sudden arrival. Ruth, however, couldn't miss the look in Everett's eyes as he stared at Lily affectionately. She burned with envy at the adoration Lily received from everyone who knew her. She wanted to love Lily too, truly, but in her core, hatred was beginning to take root.

Ruth was on her way to the post office, an errand she ran every Tuesday for her parents. The November snow had been sparse but fell liberally now. She pulled her hand-knitted scarf tighter around her face to block the sharp breeze that hit her face as she walked against the wind. She was in a rather melancholy mood the past couple of weeks since discovering Lily and Wade were meeting secretly behind her back. She confronted Wade the following day after Mrs. Stephens gave birth and he did not deny her accusations, though she questioned the reason he gave for keeping it from her; that he wanted to surprise her with his new painting.

It's not that Wade had a history of being dishonest, it was just that after what Ruth experienced with losing Noah to Lily, she was sensitive to their sudden closeness. She never had cause to doubt Wade's love previously, as he doted on her endlessly and often told her how beautiful she was, but since Lily's return to Newland she had been on edge and the revelation of their meetings had only confirmed her worst fears.

Now that Everett was back it was certain that Lily's attentions would be occupied by him and caring for her mother and baby brother, which gave her some relief, but still, she resented Lily's ability to so easily win the heart of every man she came in contact with. She wondered how Noah might feel if he knew about this current situation. Rumor had it that Lily had not yet heard from Noah and that she was growing concerned.

Maybe she will end up with Everett after all, Ruth thought smugly, all too aware of the deep love Noah had for Lily. Everyone knew it, and though she hadn't begrudged Noah the right to pursue his one true love, the possibility of Lily's happiness being thwarted somehow brought her satisfaction.

She was still deep in thought when she entered the post office and didn't notice immediately that Noah's Aunt Prissy was in the corner filling out a slip for a package she was sending out. The attendant was called over to help her through the process and dropped a stack of mail on the service counter. She apologized and told Ruth she would be back in a moment.

While Ruth waited, she happened to recognize the handwriting of the letter on top—it was Noah's. She looked back at the two ladies who were quite distracted with the forms and she decided to pick the letter up to examine it; it was postmarked from four days ago and had a return address from Florida. The attendant started heading back which caused Ruth to panic and quickly place the letter in the pocket of the satchel which hung across her chest.

Feeling flushed from the deed, she quickly collected her own mail and left the post office hastily, waving absently to Aunt Prissy, who had just noticed her and called out to say hello.

CHAPTER TWENTY-FIVE

Another two weeks had passed and still no word from Lily. Noah was becoming increasingly concerned. His restlessness was evident to Conrad as well, who tried several times to rationalize the delay. "You said she was in school, right? Maybe her studies have been keeping her busy. Maybe her letter has been lost in the mail. Maybe her family went on a trip and haven't returned yet."

None of these excuses seemed rational though. Lily was not the type of girl to be negligent of such an important communication. She was always quick to reply to his letters when she moved to Boston. And the likelihood of her only sending one letter in lieu of the several he had sent was also not likely. It didn't seem plausible that she was in any danger either for certainly one of her parents would have responded to his letters if Lily was hurt.

The true concern that crept into Noah's head was that for some reason she did not wish to continue speaking to him for some unknown reason. Even though she was the one who encouraged him to go on this trip, he wondered if she had come to resent him for it after all, especially the way in which he left her back in Boston. And then there was his greatest fear of all—was it possible she met someone else?

Noah was running these questions through his head for the millionth time as he left the post office empty-handed once again. Not even Aunt Prissy had written with any news. He decided to grab lunch at a new establishment he began frequenting since his last encounter with Sylvia. Conrad mentioned that she asked about him more than once, but Noah did not wish to return to Salty Joe's for the remainder of his stay despite Conrad's invitation to join him from time to time.

He now sat alone at a table for two in a corner of Chuck's Wagon. He quickly gave his order and was glancing casually around the room, taking notice of the haphazard décor of fishing nets, lanterns, and old faded paintings when the sound of two voices at the bar caught his attention. Two men were discussing their recent catch and one voice, in particular, struck Noah as being vaguely familiar—he couldn't quite place it, but he was sure he had heard it before.

From behind he could find no definite indication of who it might be that he would know in Key West, but continued staring in wonder, looking for any clue that might reveal his identity. The other man finally laid down some cash at the bar then got up to leave. "Good luck with that new deckhand, Marty," the man called over his shoulder as headed for the exit.

"Yup, I think he's really gonna work out, thanks for the recommendation," the man said in response.

Marty? A frightening realization washed over Noah as the identity of the stranger began to reveal itself. The man turned to wave as his friend walked out the door and Noah went cold all over as he caught sight of his profile. *That face...I do know it!* His ears, fingers and toes began tingling with a numb sensation and the sound of his own heart beating was loud in his chest. *Could it really be? Is it possible?* Yes—the man in front of him was none other than his own father, Martin Sullivan.

But how?? He continued staring straight ahead at the man's back, as if in a trance. His thoughts were interrupted when his server dropped a dirty plate in front of him with the remnants of a previous meal atop. The crash of the plate hitting the floor brought Noah to his senses long enough for him to know he had to act.

He stood, though his legs wobbled uncontrollably under him. Fighting to gain composure, he began to walk toward the figure at the bar who was now casually kicking back a brew. The closer he got, the more Noah began to tremble all over until finally, he was standing directly behind him. "Martin Sullivan?" He spoke plainly.

The man lazily turned around at the sound of his name and looked Noah up and down without any sign of recognition. "Who wants to know?"

Noah was shaken to his core but still managed to utter the words, "Me, your son, Noah."

Martin Sullivan's eyes grew wide with horror at the realization that he was found out. In a state of panic, he got up quickly from the bar and attempted to run out the door, but Noah was close on his heel, yelling for him to stop. They made it only as far as a few feet outside the entrance when Noah grabbed his father by the collar and forced him to stop and face him, man to man.

"What is going on? How is it that you are alive?" Noah demanded.

"I'm sorry," Martin replied breathlessly. "You were never supposed to know."

"Know what? That my father wasn't dead? That the man I waited for to come home and never did was living it up in Florida all this time while his only son and sister mourned? I can't believe this is actually happening!"

Barely sober and being so taken off guard by this sudden turn of events, Martin stammered over his words. "I'm sorry," he finally repeated. "I-I-I don't know what to say."

"How about you start with the truth, huh? I think you owe me that much!" Noah's temper was flaring now.

"What do you want to hear?" Martin's voice was rising as well. "I couldn't be a father, Noah, okay? I wasn't cut out for it. After your mother died I just couldn't deal with being cooped up in that house…all those memories. It was only getting harder and harder to come home every season and face you when I had nothing to give. I thought you were better off without me, okay?"

Noah was indignant at the response. "Oh really, that's your answer? That you couldn't deal with it? Well, don't expect any pity from me, *Dad*. Do you have any idea how much suffering you've caused? For all the heartbreak you experienced losing Mother, you inflicted so much more pain on us—on me. And to think I wanted to be like you once. I wanted to follow in your footsteps and be close to you. How did you do it, dad? How did you manage to deceive us? Did your boat even sink?"

Martin's voice then lowered significantly. "Yes, it did sink. Only I wasn't on it. I wasn't feeling too great that day, so I stayed behind in my shack. When news that the boat was lost and all the crew assumed dead reached me, I figured it was my chance—now or never. People assumed I was on board, so I left it at that and headed south. I didn't figure you'd ever find me out here, what with your Aunt Prissy always keeping you home. So there, you have the whole damn story. Are you happy now? Happy to find out what a bum I am? Because I don't apologize. Leaving you with your Aunt Prissy was the best thing I could do for you. She was the one who cared for you all these years. Face it, you're nothing to me...and I'm nothing to you. So, let's keep it that way, huh?"

The words were like a dagger to Noah's already fragile heart. "You know what? You're right. Leaving me to live like a prisoner with a crazy old lady was better than being raised by a devil like you. As far as I'm concerned, you went down with that ship. I never want to see your face again." Before Martin Sullivan had a chance to reply, Noah was gone, making his way back to *The Serenade* through a sea of bitter tears.

When he arrived, he found Conrad cleaning some fish

for dinner. Looking down as he focused on the task at hand he called out as he heard Noah come aboard the boat, "Hey, where ya been? Help me finish up these fish why don't ya?"

But Noah didn't reply. Instead, he threw open the hatch and jumped straight into the cabin. Conrad heard a lot of noise coming from below deck and walked over, peering down to see what the commotion was. After a moment, Noah flew up the steps in a rage.

Conrad stepped back in surprise. "What's going on kid, everything okay?"

"No, I'm not okay!" Noah wailed, then walked over the edge of the boat and tossed a pocket watch out into the clear blue waters of the marina. "Hey Conrad, maybe someone will find it someday and trade it in for a fishing net."

"What in hell was that about?" Conrad asked, quite puzzled by Noah's sudden emotional display.

"Oh nothing, just that it was my father's and I don't want anything that belonged to him. It's nothing more than trash to me now."

"Hey, hey, hey kid, what brought all this on? You might really regret that someday."

Noah shook his head emphatically. "I don't believe I will. He's truly dead to me now."

Conrad shook his head in confusion. "What's that

supposed to mean?"

"It means I hate him…" Noah's eyes burned with angry tears as his voice grew louder, "Why hasn't she written, Conrad, why? Did she abandon me too? I guess I'm not worthy of anyone's love."

Conrad reached out to grab Noah's arms. "C'mon, you need to calm down and tell me the meaning of all this."

Noah was practically hysterical now, "You wouldn't understand. Your father never abandoned you, you abandoned *him*. You left everyone you loved so how could you know what I'm going through? Now let me go!" Noah wriggled free from the weak grip on his shoulders, jumped out of the boat, and took off toward town. Conrad called after him to return, but to no avail.

The evening wore on and Conrad had no luck tracking down Noah anywhere he went. Noah had wandered the island most of the afternoon then eventually stumbled into Salty Joe's. Sylvia was not on shift but came in a bit later just as Noah had finished choking down a small pork chop and was on his fifth beer. Her eyes lit up at the sight of him and she sauntered over to where he was sitting.

"Haven't seen you around in a while," she purred, sneaking up on him. "Didn't your friend Conrad tell you I've been looking for you?"

Noah looked up and took notice of the revealing dress Sylvia was wearing; the hem was well above her knee and one strap hung loosely over her right shoulder. Her tanned skin looked like it would be smooth to the touch and her long, dark tresses smelled of sweet coconut once again.

"Have you? What for?" He asked leaning in her direction.

Sylvia wasted no time or opportunity to get close to the young, handsome boy and took a seat beside him. "I guess you could say I was hoping to get to know each other better." Her alluring accent tickled Noah's ear.

Noah was feeling a tad lightheaded and said nothing as Sylvia leaned in to nuzzle her face against his neck and kiss him lightly. "How's this for getting acquainted?" She whispered.

He looked at her directly and saw the wanton look in her flashy cat eyes. A thought suddenly came to him through the fog that this was the kind of girl Conrad had told him about. How unlike Lily Sylvia was, but right now that felt like a good thing.

Without any more hesitation, he pulled Sylvia closer and kissed her on the mouth. She was a bit stunned, to begin with, but quickly kept pace with his hungry lips. Inside, Noah was numb and didn't weigh the consequences of his impetuous actions. He thought only of pleasing himself and filling the empty hole in his heart.

Suddenly Conrad came through the door and when he caught sight of Noah and Sylvia embracing, he raced to where they were and screamed out, "What are you doing, you fool?" He slammed his hand down on the table, startling them both.

"What are you doing here, Conrad?" Noah asked angrily, embarrassed at being caught in the act of lust.

"Saving your behind from making a terrible mistake, now let's go!" He then turned to Sylvia. "And *you*, get your claws off my friend, he's spoken for."

Sylvia crossed her arms and shrugged, "I don't know who you think you are, but I think Noah here can decide for himself what he wants."

Noah added, "Conrad, this truly is none of your business, I'm gonna have to ask you to leave now."

Conrad refused, grabbed Noah's arm, and tried to force him up. "Look you're coming with me and that's all there is to it."

Noah stood up to face him and shot his friend a look of death. "I don't know who you think you are," he spat, "but you're not my father and if you think you're gonna tell me what to do, you have another thing coming."

Noah then pushed hard against Conrad to get him out of his face. Conrad stumbled back but found his footing before falling. "Look kid, I don't want to have to lay you out, but I will if you don't come to your senses."

With that, Noah attempted to slug Conrad in the jaw, connected with the side of his face, though he didn't hit him very hard before getting it right back—and Conrad didn't miss. Noah fell back into his chair and could feel blood oozing from the corner of his lip. He touched his mouth with his hand and saw red when he pulled it away.

Sylvia jumped to his side to comfort him. "Look what you did, you big oaf," she barked.

Noah pushed past Sylvia and then past Conrad and ran out into the street. Before leaving, Conrad stuck his finger in Sylvia's face, warning her once again to leave Noah alone, then bolted through the door after his friend. He watched as Noah stumbled toward the docks, realizing he wouldn't have much difficulty catching up. He decided to give him some space instead.

Finally, Noah came to a railing and put his head against the cool bar before heaving into the water below. Conrad decided to now make his move and walked over to Noah, placing his hand on his back while he spewed the rest out.

Once finished, Noah began to moan, "Why couldn't you just leave well enough alone?"

"Because you're my friend, kid, and I know girls like that will destroy your life. Girls like Lily come around once in a lifetime."

Noah slid to sit on the edge of the dock. "Yeah, well, maybe I lost her."

"You will if you keep going this way," Conrad said matter-of-factly.

Noah sighed deeply and the two sat in silence for a while before he spoke. "My father's not dead, Conrad. Turns out he faked the whole thing."

Conrad sat in stunned disbelief. "How?" was all he managed as a reply.

Noah told him the whole situation and how it went down. Conrad now understood and put his arm around his young protégé, comforting him as he grieved. His heart went out to the lad as he couldn't imagine the hurt and confusion he endured at the revelation.

"Noah," he finally said. "I know I told you I wasn't anybody's daddy, but for what it's worth, if I was, I would be proud to call you my son."

"Thank you," Noah replied. "Looks like there's an opening."

Conrad laughed. "Well, you're about the closest thing I'll probably ever have to a son, so I guess that would make two fathers that are destined to disappoint you."

Noah grinned. "Maybe, but at least one of them cared enough to keep me from going off a cliff today. Thank you, Conrad."

And with Conrad's help, Noah got up and the two of them walked back to the comfort and safety of *The Serenade* as Martin Sullivan's gold pocket watch gently settled into the sand at the bottom of the sea.

CHAPTER TWENTY-SIX

December brought more snow than Lily had seen in years. Christmas was just around the corner, but she wasn't feeling very festive. She had lost too many sleepless nights worrying about Noah and wondering why he hadn't written. Even Aunt Prissy was distressed that she too had not heard from him. Lily would do more to investigate the matter except that she had so many more responsibilities now, caring for her mother and baby brother.

Indeed, her mother had not gotten better, but was worse. Dr. Fitzgerald had been by to check on her several times, had even prescribed her an assortment of pills, but nothing helped. She came out of her room less and less. Lily was caring for little Danny almost single-handedly, with the help of friends. In spite of the problems it caused with Ruth, Lily was often thankful for the few cooking lessons she received from Wade. It helped keep them afloat as she became solely responsible for meals. She relied heavily on his cookbook as well, which she considered a godsend.

Mrs. Thomas came by less, and while she was a busy woman, Lily suspected it might have been in part due to the tensions between her and Ruth. In fact, they had spoken very little since her brother was born and the reason was quite obvious. Even in church, Ruth clung tightly to Wade's arm as if to claim him as her own possession whenever she was in close range. Lily was saddened by the estrangement between them all, feeling deep down they should have been great friends, but for the moment she had no energy to spend in that direction.

More than anything, Lily was grateful for Everett. While a part of her still felt bad about him leaving his job in Portland, she had to admit he was a tremendous help, along with his sister Flora. Her greatest contribution was raising Lily's spirits with her silly stories and general chatter, a welcome distraction from her current woes. Lily lamented how she once was able to give joy to others, but her spirits were so crushed in the last few months that she felt as though someone had turned out the light that once burned so bright within. She wondered if the day would ever come that she would get her spark back.

But if there was a change in Lily, Everett didn't seem to notice. He took as much joy as ever in making her laugh, though it was slightly more challenging these days. If anyone could, Everett was up to the task. He had changed in some ways, but was still a lovable goofball, always ready for a bit of fun, but he also put in the hours at work when he could and gave Lily money whenever he suspected she needed it. It took a great deal for Lily to set her pride aside and accept the financial help, but she relented at the thought of her baby brother and as a result, they were never without.

As for her studies, Mrs. Durgin was helping out more with Danny in the daytime so that Lily wouldn't fall behind in school. She was also permitted to take some of her schoolwork home so that she wouldn't have to put in a whole day in the classroom. She still saw Wade during that time, but aside from the occasional cordial greeting, he mostly avoided her altogether. This never ceased to sadden Lily, but she didn't have much time for friends anyway.

In the evening Everett would come over and spend time with Lily, sometimes with Flora and sometimes without.

They never really talked about much, mostly just ate dinner together and watched over Danny. One evening the snow was piling up particularly high and Everett offered to stay for the night. Lily resisted the offer and urged Everett to go home before the snow accumulated further.

After he left, she sat thinking about how nice it would be to have someone there to watch over the family. *If only that person was Noah*, she thought. Her heart was breaking but she had no one to share it with. The only time she nursed it was when everyone was down for the night and she would go in her room and cry into her pillow and pray for God to send her a sign that Noah was okay.

The following morning Lily put on her boots and long, wool coat and headed out to the market to pick up a few things for the pantry. Her mother appeared lucid enough to keep an eye on Danny for the short time she would be gone. She even smiled as she waved Lily on, assuring her all would be well.

As Lily made her way to town the snow was heavy and wet, but she managed to work her way through it swiftly enough to get to the store in a timely manner. As she entered, she shook off the flakes that had fallen along the way from her hair and coat, then looked up and to her surprise caught sight of Aunt Prissy with her husband Buck.

"Hello Priscilla!" She waved cheerfully.

Aunt Prissy was all aflutter at the sudden surprise of running into Lily. "Oh, my dear girl," she cried out. "How have you been? You know, I've been meaning to stop in and see you sometime. How is that baby brother of yours? And is your mother much better these days, I hope?"

Lily wished she had better news to share. "Danny is wonderful, Prissy, really a blessing to us, but mama is still not feeling very well I'm afraid. But I was wondering, have you by any chance received word from Noah since I last saw you?" She added, changing the subject to a more pressing matter.

Aunt Prissy frowned on both accounts. "Dear me, no, and I'm quite worried about him indeed! I was telling my husband Bucky that we simply must do something more proactive about this. We need to make sure he is okay. I knew from the beginning this whole trip wasn't a very good idea, but do young people listen to old fools like myself anymore? Of course not. Anyway, you mustn't worry much." She then leaned in to whisper loudly, "I am thinking about hiring a private investigator to check on him. Buck is all for financing the whole thing, but we mustn't tell anyone for fear of rumors spreading."

Lily brightened at the idea. "Oh really? That would be wonderful Prissy, just wonderful! I've been so heartsick over not hearing from him. It's so unlike him."

"Well, let's hope he hasn't gotten himself into too much trouble. Though you should be prepared, it could be that he's found he likes Florida so much he doesn't want to come home. There is no telling with young people. They just don't stay close to home anymore. Though I see that young Everett Durgin is back to stay. Very smart of him to have found out the importance of being home. In fact, that's where I should be heading now. I don't like to be out in all this snow. I am afraid I'll catch pneumonia if I stay out too long, but my Buck just insisted on coming down here for a few things." Buck had already wandered off and was gathering the rest of the things off their list.

Lily decided not to take Prissy's suggestion to heart, as she did mean well and there was little chance Noah had been so thoughtless by choice. "Well, Prissy, if you do hear anything, please let me know as soon as possible."

"I certainly will, dear child. And you should get home too if you know what's good for you. This cold December air is a killer, I tell ya!"

And so they parted ways, but what they didn't see was that an aisle over Ruth was shopping as well and listening to their conversation closely. Since coming upon Aunt Prissy's letter from Noah she was filled with much guilt, which was amplified all the more by overhearing the grief it was causing Lily and Prissy. Still, Ruth had thought it served Lily right. *If she hadn't tried charming my dear Wade it never would have come to this*, she thought, attempting to justify herself. But it did little to give her comfort. What choice did she have now though? If she revealed she had the letter all along she would suffer more for holding onto it so long. On the other hand, she wondered why Noah couldn't have written his aunt again.

Maybe I should write Noah and tell him what's going on. But that didn't seem like any better of an option as it was certain to uncover her deceit. *No, I think the best thing at this point is just to wait the whole thing out*, she decided.

CHAPTER TWENTY-SEVEN

The following morning Noah emerged from the boat's cabin looking and feeling tragic. As usual, Conrad was already up, sitting on the deck drinking black coffee from a tin mug and reading. "Good morning, sunshine," he called out, to which Noah simply groaned. "Want some coffee?"

Noah took the thermos from Conrad's hand, unscrewed the cap, and took a swig. The sun was glaring in his face, causing him to squint and place his hand over his eyes.

"I take it you're not feeling so hot?' Conrad asked.

"No, not really," Noah replied obviously. "I suppose I

really do have to thank you, Conrad. You kept me from doing something really stupid last night. I don't know what came over me."

"You're just hurting, kid. I know what it's like to be in that place, but I don't want to see you go down the same path I did if I can help it."

"Yes, well, it's unfortunate it took a bloody lip to get your point across. That was some right hook you got there." Noah touched the scab that had formed in the corner of his mouth overnight.

"Hey, every man should be in at least one fist fight in his life, at least I took it easy on ya." Conrad winked and then decided to change the subject. "So, what do you plan to do about everything?"

Noah groaned once more. "I don't really know. I suppose I should clear my head before making any certain plans, but I think it's time to go home. As fun as it's been, I need to find out what's going on with Lily and everything back in Newland. Besides, I don't think I could stick around here knowing my father is in the area. I don't want to see him again. He was right—he's nothing to me."

"I understand Noah, I wish I could take you home, but I have some business of my own to attend to. Anyway, I think you'll do far better if you go by train."

Noah now looked up at the blue sky overhead, "Yeah, I sure am going to miss this though."

"Miss what?"

"Sailing, the adventure of it all, seeing new places, hanging with you...*The Serenade*."

Conrad smiled, "Well, I guess it wasn't a total loss then. We sure had plenty of memorable experiences, didn't we? And I have to say, it was great having you as my first mate. You're okay, kid."

Noah spent the rest of the morning recovering from everything that happened the previous day. He hoped to make this his first and last hangover. His heart ached as he played the words his father had said to him over in his mind. *How am I going to break the news to Aunt Prissy?* He wondered.

By mid-afternoon, Noah was feeling well enough to head into town to purchase a train ticket to Boston. He decided to give himself a couple more days to prepare for the journey and to make sure he tied up any loose ends with Conrad. He stopped at the post office on his way back to the boat and was disappointed to find there was no letter once again. He considered whether he should write Lily and Aunt Prissy once more to alert them of his pending arrival. *Would Lily even care?* But ultimately, he thought better of it, realizing he would arrive much sooner than the letters would. Instead, he decided to head back to the boat to begin preparing for his departure.

Lily came home from the market, her arms heavy with the sacks she filled. Trudging through the snow was a greater chore going home due to carrying her purchases and by now the hem of her wool coat was wet from the journey there and back. She went into the kitchen to set down her packages then walked over to her mother's room to check and see how she and Danny were getting along without her.

When she entered, she saw her mother holding little Danny and rocking contentedly while she sang him a sweet lullaby. She didn't look up when Lily entered but continued singing softly. Lily sat on the edge of the bed and was pleased to see all was well during her brief absence. The song her mother was singing was familiar. It was a lullaby she sang to her as a child. The melody soothed her soul as she listened quietly.

Sleep my baby on my bosom
Warm and cozy will it prove
Round thee mother's arms are folding
In her heart a mother's love

There shall no one come to harm thee
Naught shall ever break thy rest
Sleep my darling babe in quiet
Sleep on mother's gentle breast

Sleep serenely, baby, slumber
Lovely baby, gently sleep
Tell me wherefore art thou smiling
Smiling sweetly in thy sleep?

Do the angels smile in heaven
When thy happy smile they see?
Dost thou on them smile while slumb'ring
On my bosom peacefully

Do not fear the sound of a breeze
Brushing leaves against the door
Do not dread the murmuring seas
Lonely waves washing the shore

Sleep child mine, there's nothing here
While in slumber at my breast
Angels smiling, have no fear
Holy angels guard your rest

When she completed the song, she continued to hum the melody lightly, so Lily got up, snuck back out the door, and went back to the kitchen to put the rest of her purchases away. She wondered what made her mother think of that old song. She hadn't heard it in years, but it brought back so many precious memories of her youth.

Seeing her mother tenderly rocking her baby brother gave her hope that perhaps she was beginning to come back to them. Was it possible her mother was finally getting better? *How wonderful it would be to feel like a family again*, she thought smiling to herself. Perhaps her father would even be able to join them sooner than imagined. Then all would be right in the world. *And what about Noah?*

Her heart held out hope for him too, though the prospect was growing dimmer by the day, save for Aunt Prissy's suggestion to hire an investigator. She couldn't think too much about their conversation though. For now, she longed to enjoy this moment of peace, so once she finished up her chores, Lily spent the rest of the afternoon catching up on her studies.

When the transition to evening began to surface, she got up from her little desk and stretched before heading into the kitchen to get dinner ready. Everett and Flora would be joining them tonight, which she was looking forward to. She hoped her mother would be feeling well enough to join them too.

Her mother would occasionally sit with them at supper, though she ate very little and said even less. It still brought Lily some solace knowing that she was making the effort. Somehow it gave her assurance that in time she would adjust to their new reality. For the time being she heard no sound coming from her mother's room, so she decided to let her mother rest until their guests arrived.

Tonight, she was making one of her favorite dishes—a whole chicken with roasted vegetables and biscuits with homemade strawberry preserves for dessert. It was a modest, but tasty meal that never failed. She had just begun to set the table when there was a knock at the door. Lily opened it to find Everett had come alone and was carrying a pot with a three-foot evergreen.

"Come in," she waved, "It sure is cold out there!"

Everett stepped into the entryway and shook the snow from his coat that had been coming down lightly. "Yes, I should say so! Flora will be along shortly, I just wanted to bring this." He placed the pot in Lily's hands which caused a wide grin to spread across her face.

"What's this all about?"

Everett gave his classic lopsided grin. "I thought with the holiday coming up it might add a bit of cheer."

Lily thanked him then took the little tree into the kitchen to give it some water, then continued with her dinner prep. Everett followed behind to find out how things were coming along.

"Wow it really smells great in here," he commented. "You sure have come a long way in your cooking skills."

Lily blushed as she went to stir the pot that was simmering on the stove. "I'm really not that great, but I'm glad if you think I'm improving. Wade's cookbook has gone a long way in helping me try new things. I am making a special homemade gravy for tonight." She turned around to find Everett close behind her. He leaned over her shoulder to get a look at the gravy she was making.

"Mmm looks delicious." Lily felt tingles go up her spine from him being pressed so close to her. Suddenly Lily felt uncomfortable in his presence even though they had maintained a great friendship. Everett was always especially good at making her laugh, but since coming home from

Portland she noticed that many of his childish antics had diminished. She wasn't sure if it was maturity or something else, but his serious side surfaced more often than ever before. Right now she could go for a bit of his silly humor.

"You know what we should do?" Lily suggested in an attempt to lighten the mood. "We should play a little trick on Flora when she gets here. She loves that sort of thing. Any ideas?"

Everett was in no mood to fool around. He was hoping to use this opportunity alone with Lily to talk to her about more serious matters. "Probably not tonight, Lily," he replied. "Flora didn't strike me as being in a playful mood this evening. The reason she is coming later is that she's been doing so poorly in school, so mother and father are making her study more in the evenings to get her grades up. Her teachers say she spends too much time socializing and now she is threatening to quit upon the first marriage proposal that comes along. My parents are still urging her to finish out the year at the very least. Let's face it, Flora has never been very bright, or the type of girl interested in getting an education, but we all want to encourage her to keep at it."

Lily was sad to hear about Flora's struggles and decided to drop the idea. Instead, she turned the topic to Everett's future. "And what about you? Any thoughts of continuing your own education? I'm sure it would be a real benefit to you while you have the freedom to do so."

"No, I was made to work with my hands. I don't think I'm good for much else. Besides, I don't actually feel free at the moment. I want to be here for you as long as you need the support, Lily." He placed a reassuring hand on her shoulder, which made Lily's heart quicken.

To stifle her nerves, Lily grabbed a hand towel on the counter and began fidgeting with it. "Everett, you know I can't ask you to give up your future for me. I mean, I couldn't be more thankful for all you've done for us during these really difficult times, but mama's getting better and soon Noah will be home, and well, I don't feel it would be right to hold you back from doing something more."

"Will he?"

"Will he what?" Lily's eyes narrowed.

"Will Noah be home soon? Because it looks to me, he hasn't reached out to anyone since he's been in Florida and there's no telling what his plans are. Is that really what you want to bank your hopes on?"

Lily turned away from Everett and back to the stove. "Noah won't let me down. I am certain he has a good explanation for why he hasn't written."

"Does he? Because you don't sound like you believe

that. I mean, he could be dead for all we know," he said insensitively, planting further seeds of doubt.

Lily whipped around to face Everett, her eyes flashing. "How could you say such a thing?"

"I'm sorry, Lily, but you know we're all thinking it. Let's get real here. He may never come home and then what?"

Lily placed her face in the towel she was still holding. "I can't think about that right now. As long as there is still a chance…" She turned around once again to hide her tears, resisting the temptation to entertain such terrible thoughts.

Everett came up behind her and put his arms around her for comfort. "I'm sorry Lily," he said softly. "I didn't want to hurt you. It's just that…I don't want to see you struggle anymore. I want you to know you are cared for. Will you look at me?" Lily shook her head; she couldn't face him yet. "Please? There's something I want to ask you."

Lily stood firm. "Please don't, Everett."

"I must. I can't keep pretending that my motives here have been altruistic. You know I love you, Lily, I always have. Please look at me."

Lily reluctantly turned around to face her dear friend. She owed him that much when he had been there for her so faithfully in her time of need.

"Lily," Everett implored, taking the towel from her

hands and wiping her eyes. "I want to marry you. I want to take care of you. I know I don't have much to offer right now, but I'll work hard to provide everything you need."

Lily looked into Everett's worn, pleading eyes and her heart was touched by his offer. But before she could answer a knock came at the door, which was certain to be Flora. Lily excused herself, feeling secretly grateful for the sudden interruption. She wiped her eyes again quickly and answered the door with a forced smile. "Come in, my dear girl!" She said emphatically to Flora. "Dinner is just about ready. Go on ahead into the dining room. I just have to go get Mama and we'll eat soon."

Flora took off her overcoat and hung it on the rack near the door and bounded into the dining room. Lily could hear Everett greeting his sister and she let out a sigh of relief. She entered her mother's room and saw she was still fast asleep. She walked over to her bedside and nudged her gently. "Mama," she whispered. "Dinner's almost ready." But her mother didn't budge. There was no movement whatsoever. Her lips were a bluish hue and an empty bottle lay next to her.

Lily shrieked in horror then ran haphazardly toward the dining room in a state of total panic, calling out Everett and Flora's name.

Everett met her halfway. "What on earth is it?" He

exclaimed at the sight of her white, ashen face.

"It's Mama, it's Mama…go get Dr. Fitzgerald right away!"

CHAPTER TWENTY-EIGHT

It was a bleak and frigid winter morning. No trace of light from the sun managed to break through the slate-gray sky. Wispy flakes drifted softly to the snow-covered ground. Lily stood staring at the vault in the cemetery which held her mother's body until it could be put in the ground with the spring thaw. Mrs. Thomas was holding little Danny, who was snugly wrapped in a double layer of blankets, while Reverend Thomas spoke the words he had said hundreds of times before. "Blessed are they that mourn, for they shall be comforted…" Lily heard nothing except the howling wind whistling in her uncovered ears. She was numb now. Her thoughts were as vacant as the sea in winter.

Everett came alongside Lily and took her hand in a show of support. She neither pulled away nor squeezed his hand in return. She allowed it for his sake more than her own. She didn't need comfort—not yet anyway. It still wasn't real to her, even as she looked upon the tomb that held her mother's casket. Surely it contained a secret tunnel that led to the blue cottage, where her mother would be back in her bed, awaiting their return.

The service ended and several friends, family, and relative strangers approached Lily with hugs and condolences. She accepted them graciously but said little in return. "The poor little one. No father or mother." She heard one lady whisper about her baby brother. "It's a shame she'll have to quit her schooling for sure now. Such a smart girl too." Another said of Lily. Harshest of all was the one who said, "It's all the father's fault for leaving his dear wife to care for the children alone. Any woman in that circumstance would do the same."

Lily wished to flee from all the sympathetic gazes, but she was frozen in place, looking down, down, down. Any moment now she would awaken from this nightmare and return to the family she once knew; her father would be sitting in his favorite armchair reading a book from his library and her mother would be humming little ditties as she peeled vegetables for dinner in the kitchen. She need only click her heels together three times to return home.

Suddenly the sound of a baby's cry interrupted her thoughts. She looked over to see Danny's face red with all the concerns of a newborn. He didn't exist in her perfect memories but was all she needed to motivate her to move forward into the future.

Lily walked over to Mrs. Thomas and offered to take the baby from her arms. She hesitated, only to receive reassurance from Lily that she was in a state to handle him just now. "It's fine, Mrs. Thomas," Lily said in reply to her kind concern. "He's my responsibility now. We must go home."

"Understandable dear," Mrs. Thomas agreed. "It's been a long couple days for you and the baby, perhaps you should go home at that. But please, my dear, do not hesitate to call on us if you need assistance. Will you be going alone?"

Everett jumped in. "My sister and I will see Miss Stephens home. It will be alright, thank you Mrs. Thomas for all your help, but she will be in good hands."

Mrs. Thomas nodded and the three of them headed back to the blue cottage to get little Danny down for a nap.

Danny continued to fuss the rest of the way home, but

once they arrived, Lily quickly tended to his need for milk and a fresh change of clothes. She rocked him by the fire while he ate and soon, he drifted into a peaceful sleep. *How fortunate that he does not understand what has been taken from him,* Lily thought. If only she too could be at such peace. No, the worst task of all was still before her. She had not yet had a chance to inform her father of his wife's passing. Everything happened so quickly, but tomorrow she would have to break the horrible news.

For today she wanted nothing more than to rest after entertaining so many well-meaning visitors. The house was quiet now as Everett, and even dear Flora, gave her the space she needed to settle down. Lily was equally glad for their company *and* their silence. She wasn't ready to face the empty cottage alone just yet. Without her even having to say a word Everett reassured her that he and Flora would stay for as many nights as she would like. She nodded and thanked them as Flora went into the kitchen to make them all a bit of lunch.

Everett sat close in the chair next to Lily. "Are you doing okay?" He asked for the twentieth time that day.

"Yes, I am as well as can be expected, thank you for asking," Lily replied in similar fashion as before. "I'm just going to need time to figure things out."

"Well, my offer is still on the table, Lily. You don't

have to give me an answer now, but I want you to know, nothing has changed. I will be here for you and the baby. You need never be alone."

"Thank you," Lily said simply.

"There is one thing though," he added cautiously. "I got a job offer in Portland. I just found out yesterday afternoon, but I didn't want to trouble you with all you had going on. I don't start until next week, but I'll have to leave soon. I hope you and Danny will join me."

Lily was astonished at this sudden development. "So soon?" She inquired.

"I'm sorry it's so sudden, but it's a great opportunity. Not to mention I thought it might be good for you to make a new start under the circumstance."

"I-I-I-don't know if I can make a decision like that so quickly. I care for you Everett, honestly, but you must know..."

Everett hung his head. "Yes, it's Noah. I know. Well, I can't make that choice for you, Lily, but you can either decide to be with the one who is here for you now or wait around for someone who may never return. The last thing I want to do is pressure you, and if you really want me to, I will pass up the job while you think things over, but I see no reason for us to sit around here waiting for who knows how long on a completely unknown factor."

Lily looked into the fire, stone faced. "I just can't say right now. I'm sorry."

Everett reached out to touch her hand. "You don't have to make a decision right now, but if you could please let me know in a couple of days I would like to write to accept or reject the offer."

"Regardless of what I choose Everett, you must accept the job. Please, I insist."

"Whatever you wish," he softly replied. Everett knew that now was not the time to argue.

Relaying the news of her mother's death to her father was harder than she anticipated. Everett waited outside for Lily while she went in to see him. She originally thought to go alone but was now glad she had support. As soon as she saw Everett's face, she ran to him, flung herself into his arms, and sobbed. Everett held her tightly, not prodding her before she was ready. After a time, Lily finally wiped the tears from her eyes and made an effort to compose herself before speaking.

"He didn't take it very well," she said finally. "I've never seen him look so broken. Oh Everett, I barely recognized him at all. He has lost so much weight and there is a wild look in his eyes. I don't know if he truly understood how bad off Mama was these past months. I hated to leave him alone with such terrible news. He blames himself and I'm worried about what he might do. Did I do the right thing in coming here?"

Everett put his arm around Lily's shoulder. "Someone had to tell him and it was better coming from you. At least you were the one. At least he wasn't alone when he found out."

Lily nodded in agreement. "Yes, I know you're right, it was better this way. I just wish I could have been there for him longer. He is so lonely and unloved in that place and it shows. He won't tell me much about how things have been going because I think he doesn't want to worry me, but Everett, I am deeply concerned for him." She paused a moment. "We talked about Danny too. He asked if I was able to handle caring for him and I told him I have been doing so practically since he was born. He wants me to continue raising him as my own and gave his blessing to officially adopt him as soon as I'm married."

Everett interjected. "I'm going to assume he didn't

mean to me. You didn't tell him about Noah, did you?"

Lily turned away, speaking in a hushed tone. "No. I just didn't want to worry him further. Right now he believes everything is set and..."

"And it is if you want it to be," Everett finished her sentence. "Marry me and come to Portland, Lily. You know it's the best thing for you both."

Lily didn't respond but left Everett's statement hanging in the air. For now, she could think of nothing else except going home and getting some rest. She knew she was running out of options and that only a foolish, stubborn girl would turn down this offer from Everett, her dear friend—especially under such circumstances. She was aware of the fact that she was fortunate to have him by her side, having given up so much already to be there for her in her time of need, but for at least one more day she wanted to hold out hope that Noah was not lost to her forever.

When Everett dropped her off at the door of the Blue Cottage he offered to stay, but Lily refused. "I need time to think," she said simply.

Everett persisted only slightly, then gave into her wishes. Lily was stubborn when she made up her mind, but he also acknowledged it probably was a good idea for her to think things through. The sooner she let him know, the better. Not to mention, he had some thinking of his own to do.

Once alone, Lily laid her baby brother down in his bassinet and rocked him gently until he fell asleep. She stared down at his peaceful little face and the realization struck her that he now belonged to her—she was a mother. It had not occurred to her to think of it until this very moment, but for all intents and purposes, she was all he had in the world. He needed to be cared for properly and Lily knew that wasn't something she could offer him alone.

Lily went to her mother's bedside and fell to her knees beside it. For the first time since her mother's death, she felt her absence keenly and realized how truly alone she was. She had been in a daze but was now filled with fear and desperation as she looked out to a bleak future without Noah. She buried her face in the quilt and wept bitterly. "Dear God," she cried out. "Please help me! I don't know what to do. I need your guidance. I will marry Everett if you want me to, but I love Noah and I don't know how to stop loving him. Where is he? Why has he not written? Please, show me what to do." She waited silently, half expecting the voice of God to answer, but there was no reply.

It was as if the silence was her answer. Her once sparkling spirit had been crushed, but this time for good. She wondered if she would ever feel joy again. She spent the rest of her day mourning the loss of her innocence and seeking the strength to let go of the ideals she clung to so desperately, including the dear boy she loved so completely. It would not come easily.

She wandered over to her own bedroom and entered it, noting how it was the room of a child, but she was no longer that little girl. Her eyes instinctively landed on Noah's masterful painting of her by the sea. She gazed at it often, but how long ago that day seemed now. How much had changed. She thought back to his plans of creating a painting studio for the two of them one day. How perfectly lovely the idea was and yet how impossible it seemed now.

She heard Danny begin to stir and went back to his bassinet. She scooped him up and swaddled him tightly in a warm blanket. She promptly put on her winter coat and boots and wandered into the snowy trees and along the covered path that led to Birchwood Cottage. It seemed like ages since she had last laid eyes upon it, what with the winter weather and her days occupied with the responsibility of caring for her mother and baby brother.

The snow fell heavy as she exited the covering of the treetops. There it was—as stony and stately as it ever was, but empty. She looked to the window in Noah's sitting room where he first peered out at her and waved. And the terrace where they first formally met. How like children they were then. She thought of his boyish, toothy grin and cool blue eyes. How he had stared at her with an enchanted gaze. Even when they fought there was no question in Lily's mind that Noah cared for her. *Did he still?*

She now looked out to the frozen sea and could barely remember what it looked like in summer. She closed her eyes and tried to remember the sound of waves crashing over the sandy beach and the warm sun beating on her bare shoulders as she gathered shells along the shore. She remembered how that day in the painting felt. Little did she know how Noah had watched her with such adoration, captivated by her every move that would one day lead to the masterpiece now in her possession.

Danny began to cry and broke the illusion of her daydream. She pressed the baby close to her chest and took one final look at the cottage which represented a past she couldn't hold onto and a future she had to release. "Goodbye, Noah," she whispered against the icy draft whirling along the coast. Her farewell scattered to the wind, along with her hopes. She turned and headed back to the blue cottage, a part of her soul left for dead at the edge of the sea where Birchwood Cottage mournfully stood, dark and lonely.

CHAPTER TWENTY-NINE

Noah stepped off the train at the station in Boston and wasted no time. He headed to Lily's house without bothering to stop for a bite to eat. In short order, he would be face to face with his darling girl. All his questions about why she hadn't responded to his letters no longer mattered. All he could think of was taking her into his arms and kissing her sweet lips. That moment couldn't come soon enough.

What a change of scenery Boston was from Key West. The snow was coming heavy but it didn't stop Noah from rushing through the city streets, flying past the sea of towering brownstones. They all looked so similar but only one held his future bride. Her front door was before him now. It need only to open and reveal her familiar friendly face to eliminate all the cares of the past few months. He strutted up the steps, gave a hearty knock, and waited. A few moments passed when he heard the shuffling of someone coming to answer. The door opened but the face before him was neither familiar nor friendly.

"May I help you?" A man in a suit asked, who was clearly a butler.

"Is Lily Stephens home? I must see her right away!" Noah answered eagerly.

The man looked Noah up and down doubtfully. "I'm sorry sir, but you must have the wrong place. There is nobody residing here by that name."

He almost shut the door when Noah interjected, "You must be mistaken! Isn't this the Stephens's place? I am sure of it."

The Butler did not relent. "I am sorry, but this is not, in fact, the Stephens residence, it is the Callahan's. Perhaps you have the wrong address?"

Noah consulted the paper Lily had given him with the address once again and confirmed. He then looked at the chandelier behind the man and recognized it immediately. "No sir, this is certainly the right house. I don't understand what's happened though."

The butler eased up a bit at the sight of Noah's confusion. "I do apologize if there has been some sort of mix-up, sir. The Callahan's have not been here more than a couple of months. Perhaps they know something about the Stephens family you are searching for. Please come in and wait while I ask the master."

Noah was happy to come in out of the cold and entered the home upon the man's invitation. He held out a hand offering Noah a seat then disappeared down a hallway. Noah waited patiently for his return, his mind reeling with questions as to what could have happened to Lily and her family since he was gone. She had not mentioned any plans to move. In fact, her father and mother had seemed quite settled in.

A few minutes later the butler returned with another man at his side. "This is Mr. Callahan," he introduced the man. "I believe he may be able to help answer your questions."

Noah stood and shook the man's hand, repeating his question to the stranger. "Mr. Callahan, thank you for speaking with me. I am looking for the Stephens family who resided here when I visited in September. Can you tell me where they went?"

"I'm sorry son, I do not know where they've gone, I only know that a Stephens family did indeed live here and left very hastily. I have no other information about them, except that I did continue to get their mail sometime before informing the post office of the change of address. I handed over all their letters and parcels to them to manage and know nothing else. So, I recommend you check with the post office to see if perhaps they left a forwarding address."

Noah couldn't immediately make sense of this unexpected turn of events but thanked the man for the help he was able to offer, got directions to the nearest post office, then left him to return to whatever activity he was called away from. As he stepped back out onto the wintry street, he didn't know whether or not he should be worried. He was only certain that he had to get to the bottom of this as quickly as possible, only it was getting late in the afternoon.

By the time Noah arrived at the post office he saw it was closed for the day, which meant he would need to get a room and check back again in the morning. He wandered further into town to see if a vacancy was available. He figured it probably wouldn't be too difficult to secure a place this time of year, but it was incredibly cold, and he wished to do so as soon as possible. He walked among the snow drifts that covered the sidewalks which had yet to be shoveled. His feet were numb with cold as he hadn't packed properly for a New England winter. The bitter wind nipped at his nose and cheeks until they were raw. The only warmth he found was in the beauty of the city richly decorated for the holidays. The smell of pine was pleasing, as was the soft glow of the city lights before him.

After booking a modest room, Noah decided to grab a bit of dinner before heading to bed. It was dark now, but he didn't have to wander far from the boarding house to find an inviting tavern. A warm meal and a cold drink sounded like it would sustain him on that frigid night. Noah entered the dimly lit establishment and found it was quite crowded, though it was still too early to be very rowdy. He found a seat at a little table in the center of the room and put in his order.

His food came out quickly and Noah was halfway through his meal when suddenly a hand gripped him on the shoulder from behind. He was startled by the sudden contact and turned around to a familiar voice which proclaimed, "Hey, ain't you the kid who was with that pathetic excuse of a sailah? I had a feeling you'd be back." Noah's eyes widened with horror at the sight of Smitty and two of his thuggish friends standing on either side of him.

His first instinct was to run, but Smitty's bear paw-like hand held him firmly in his seat against the struggle. "Oh no you don't, we got you this time kid. Smitty don't never fahget nobody who wronged him. I think you'd better come with us. We'd hate to make a scene."

Noah was frantic, his mind reeling with what he might say to get out of this terrible predicament. "Look, Smitty, is it? I don't know what you want with me. I don't want any trouble and I had nothing whatsoever to do with the situation you're referring to."

"Maybe you did and maybe you didn't," Smitty replied scratching his prickly chin. "But I bet you ten to one you know where I can find that scamp."

"He's not here in Boston anymore, honest." Noah's voice cracked. "He sailed south for the winter months. I am just trying to go back home to see my girl. I can't do anything for you."

Smitty looked at Noah and then to his friends who were awaiting his orders. "I don't know if I believe you, so just the same, I think you better come with us."

Noah reacted as a panicked bird caught in a cage. Without much thinking, he shook himself free and ran toward the bar in hopes of escaping out the back door of the establishment. He didn't get very far though before one of Smitty's thugs grabbed hold of his shirt and pulled him back, almost causing Noah to fall backward. Fortunately, his momentum was great enough to tear the shirt so that he didn't lose his footing. Instead, he turned around to see a fist flying toward him, to which he was able to duck quickly to avoid and miss the impact. The thug lunged forward into the bar and gave Noah a chance to escape once again.

However, another one of Smitty's thugs was hot on his heels and managed to successfully seize Noah's arm. This time when Noah turned around, he was faced with Smitty, who grabbed him by the collar and gave him a blow to the chin. Noah fell against a chair and regained his composure enough to grab it and throw it at the two burly men. It didn't make direct impact but caused them to both step back and give Noah enough space to grab another chair and throw it at them. This time he hit Smitty, who fell to the ground, so he grabbed another chair and attempted to do the same to his friend. His friend, however, grabbed the leg of the chair before he could throw it and the two struggled over it before suddenly there was a loud commotion, accompanied by a sharp whistle.

The police had been summoned just outside the tavern and now the four of them were being cuffed and detained by Boston's finest. Smitty fought hardest against the officer's grip but eventually succumbed to his inevitable arrest. Noah didn't yet feel the pain in his jaw and thought of nothing except the inconvenience this would cause as he was taken to the jailhouse with Smitty and his gang. His spirits fell with the realization that he would likely have to wait even longer to find out where Lily was.

Ruth was looking forward to the afternoon. Christmas was in two days and Wade was coming over to have tea with her family and she was excited to give him his gift—a new cookbook that the lady at the bookshop recommended for Italian cuisine. Wade had shown a great deal of interest recently in trying some Italian recipes, so Ruth was eager to give it to him.

Things between them had been tense for a while there following Ruth's revelation of the time Wade was spending with Lily, but all that was behind them now. Lily had been wildly preoccupied since Everett's arrival and now with caring for her little brother in lieu of her mother's tragic death. Ruth pitied Lily now, seeing how far she had fallen from the high-spirited girl she once knew who charmed everyone she came in contact with, but secretly she found some satisfaction in the knowledge that Noah had deserted her and she would likely be forced to marry Everett. People spoke of nothing else since her mother's passing.

Ruth was mostly just glad that she no longer had to worry about Lily being a threat where Wade was concerned. It took a little time, but Wade had come back around to doting on Ruth as he once did before Lily's return to town. Wade may have denied having feelings for Lily, but she was taking no chances. Wade was unhappy with Ruth's insistence that he no longer speak to Lily, but given time, he got over his displeasure regarding the ultimatum. Yes, they were back to being quite a couple in love and Ruth was certain to receive a proposal any time now.

Wade arrived in his usual punctual manner. Ruth eagerly rushed to give him his present and watched with great anticipation as he pulled at the pretty paper she so carefully wrapped it with. The delighted expression on Wade's face was all Ruth needed to feel she had chosen well. He then handed Ruth her gift, to which Ruth opened quickly to find a sparkling red brooch. She was breathless with excitement at the beauty of it, exclaiming how well it would go with the new scarf she knit.

"I must show mother, Wade, wait here!" She said. The sound of Ruth speaking to her mother about the "oh-so-lovely" brooch could be heard from the sitting room and it pleased Wade to see Ruth so happy. *She is a beautiful girl who should be well decorated at all times*, he thought.

Just then Ruth poked her head out the door. "Tea is just about to be served," she called to him. "Oh, I almost forgot, I picked up some shortbread cookies for all of us to share. They are in my satchel; will you please be a dear and grab them?" Ruth disappeared behind the door again.

Wade stood to grab Ruth's satchel and reached into it, feeling the box, and pulled it out. Along with it came a letter that was stuck to the underside, which fell to the floor in front of him. Wade bent down to pick it up when he noticed that it was addressed to Priscilla Simmons. He knew her to be Noah's Aunt Prissy, so he was immediately curious and examined it further. The return address was from Florida.

"What is this?" He called to Ruth, who was now in the doorway urging him to join them.

"What?" She asked unaware.

"This letter…why do you have it?"

Ruth went white and began to stammer, "Oh that…that's nothing. Here, I meant to deliver it today and forgot."

She walked over to grab it out of his hand, but Wade pulled it back. "Wait a minute, the postmark on this date is from weeks ago. And it's already open."

Ruth tried once again to pull it from his hand but failed to do so. "Please give it to me Wade, it's nothing, really."

Wade frowned deeply and began opening it against Ruth's persistent protests. He read the contents to himself then looked up at Ruth with new eyes. "How could you do this, Ruth?" It was as though the spell she had over him was broken in an instant.

"Do what?" She played innocent.

"You know very well. How did you get this letter?"

"I found it on the road and meant to return it to Mrs. Simmons. Someone from the post office must have dropped it." She lied.

"I don't believe you," Wade said with an accusing stare. "How could you do this to your friends? And with everyone worrying about Noah and his whereabouts. Some have even thought he might be dead! And you knew all this time and said nothing?"

Ruth was deeply embarrassed to be caught red-handed in her deception. She knew she was trapped and couldn't wiggle her way out of the situation. Her only option was to appeal to Wade's mercy. "I'm sorry, Wade," she cried. "I know it wasn't the right thing to do. I panicked, okay? You have no idea how much it hurt when Lily took Noah away from me. I was afraid she would take you too. I love you…"

But Wade wasn't taking the bait. "That makes no sense, Ruth. How would keeping Noah and Lily apart prevent me from pursuing her? No, I think you wanted to get revenge. You were hoping she wouldn't find out so you could drive them apart. I suppose you thought she would have no choice but to marry Everett given her predicament?"

Ruth was sobbing uncontrollably now. "I know it was wrong, I just couldn't take it back. I regretted it immediately, but I knew everyone would know what I did. Wade, forgive me, my love!" She pleaded.

"I can't even look at you," Wade said as he marched for the door, letter in hand. "I am delivering this to its rightful owner this instant."

Ruth ran to him, grabbing his arm to keep him from leaving. "Oh Wade, how could you? How could you think nothing of dragging my name through the mud? And for what? A girl you claim you didn't love? How can I believe you ever cared for me?"

Wade shook her hand from his arm. "The truth is Ruth, I did love you, more than you can ever know—I'm sure I still do—but this thing you did is too terrible for words. It has ruined everything. So now I must make this right, though I will do my best to protect your reputation as much as the situation will allow. That's all I can promise. As for you and me, I'm afraid we're through as I can see no way back from this." Wade took one look back at Ruth's pitiful face before he headed out the door. The grief that ensued was unbearable, but she left him no choice. The last thing Wade heard was Ruth wailing for him to come back, but it was too late. He was a man on a mission.

CHAPTER THIRTY

Lily finished packing her belongings—the things she would need for the time being. The rest she would leave at the blue cottage until she could return in the spring. Then she would decide what to do with the charming little home that had become so dear to her heart. One thing was certain, she could not bear to ever live there again, so close to the home of the one who had seemingly forsaken her.

She replayed the scene in her mind from early that morning. She had risen with the sun and had dutifully fed little Danny, then dressed for Everett's arrival. She expected him at ten, but he arrived at nine. She was ready well before then, so it made no difference. *Better to get the inevitable over with*, she thought.

"Sit down." She motioned to Everett to have a seat in her father's chair. "I'm ready to give you an answer."

"I think I'd rather stand," Everett replied, his hands shaking and moist with perspiration. Just before Lily opened her mouth to speak Everett interrupted her. "Wait, before you give me your answer there is something you must know. I am aware that it may make a difference in how you wish to answer, but I didn't feel it would be fair to withhold the truth from you. I want you to make this decision free and clear."

Lily nodded, somewhat taken back by this sudden revelation to come. She had rehearsed her speech well and would now have to hold her tongue a while longer. "Go ahead, I'm listening," she replied.

Everett paced back and forth several times before stopping. "Alright, here is the truth of the matter, Lily. I didn't wish to deceive you, but I believe you may be under false assumptions as to why I've come back to Newland. Yes, I did wish to return to be there for you in your time of need, but things weren't quite what they appeared either. I guess you could say I was too embarrassed at the time to tell the truth about the real reason I left Portland, but now I feel I owe you that much under the circumstance. It's true that I was working in the shipyards and the owner offered to take me on after my apprenticeship. What I didn't tell you was that I blew it." Everett swallowed hard. "I didn't take the work seriously and I fooled around a lot on the job, laughing with the other guys. I enjoyed my sudden freedom in Portland and was having all these new experiences. I started staying out late carousing, sometimes until the early morning, and acting like an ass in general. I was late to work often, even too sick to come in at times, so eventually, I was let go."

"I'll never forget the look of disappointment when my boss told me had to cut me loose—that it was a tough decision since they saw so much potential in me to be a good worker, but that I had let them down one too many times. I was a screw-up, Lily, I know that and take full responsibility. And I've learned my lesson. But coming back to Newland when I did was fortunate timing. Seeing you again was like looking into the sun after being underground for a year. You made me realize what was at stake for my childish ways and I suddenly had a new sense of purpose—to make things right by being there for you and Danny. I'm really sorry if I misled you, but my feelings for you have always been true. However, if your answer is no, then I want you to know there is no reason to feel guilty for some perceived sacrifice I made on your behalf. You owe me nothing."

Lily took a seat to think over all that Everett had revealed to her. Her prepared speech was now out the window, in light of this new information. On the one hand, it did relieve her of a sense of obligation to Everett, but in light of her circumstance, it made his offer no less appealing. After a time of contemplation, she looked up into Everett's eyes and said, "Okay."

"Okay?" Everett echoed.

"Okay. I'll still marry you, Everett Durgin."

Everett couldn't believe his ears. "You will?"

Lily nodded as a slight smile spread across her lips. Everett's honesty had convinced her that she could live with the decision being her own. Her heart was breaking over Noah, but she also knew Everett loved her and that they could have a good life together. And Danny needed a father.

Everett scooped her into his arms and hugged her tightly. "We have no time to lose then! Our train leaves tonight, so you better start packing if we wish to be on it."

"So soon?" Lily asked.

"I'm sorry darling, but yes, we should leave right away. We can celebrate Christmas in Portland—as man and wife—imagine that!"

Before Lily could respond to the hasty proposition, Everett was like his old boyish self again, full of energy and laughter. Even Lily found herself brimming with optimism as he detailed their plans for the next couple of days and talked of how excited Flora would be about gaining Lily as a sister. "It's going to be great," he reassured her. "You'll see!" He placed a kiss on her forehead before taking off to tell his family of the forthcoming plans and to gather up his own belongings.

Three hours passed and now Lily was snapping her suitcase shut with the last of her and Danny's essentials. She had spent some of the morning doing her best to ensure that everything was in proper order for her departure from the blue cabin. She didn't know how long it would be until she would return but felt good that she had covered all her bases.

As she did a final walk-through of the house she stopped at her bedroom. She surveyed the contents she was leaving behind one final time—all the things that would remind her of childhood days. The innocence was gone forever, and it was time to grow up. Her eyes once again landed on the painting from Noah, which hung proudly on her wall—a constant reminder of his love. It represented the hope that he would return for her. How had she forsaken their love in such a short time?

She then decided to look through her own paintings one final time. Lily knew that such a pastime would be a luxury she couldn't afford in the city, not to mention it would not be compatible with her life with Everett. She thought back on the first time she shared her work with Everett and how he had seemed impressed enough. He had said her work was "good enough to be in comic books." Lily knew he meant it as a compliment, but he didn't understand art. That was something she and Noah shared and it wouldn't be fair to bring that into a new marriage. Her heart grieved once again over the loss of something dear to her but felt she had no choice but to leave it all behind.

After shedding one final tear over this great loss, Lily carefully closed the door to her bedroom and her old life. She expected Everett to come back any time now and jumped when she heard a sudden knock at the door. "Coming, Everett!" She called out, but was surprised to see none other than Aunt Prissy at her threshold. She was suddenly embarrassed and wondered whether word of her pending marriage to Everett had traveled so quickly as to prompt the unexpected visitor.

"I'm sorry, were you expecting someone else, my dear? Because there is something I simply *must* tell you." Aunt Prissy was all a-flutter and clearly ignorant of Lily's forthcoming plan.

Lily's heart began beating fast against her chest in anticipation of what news she came to deliver. "What is it

Prissy? Please tell me! Have you heard from Noah?"

"As a matter of fact, I have, my dear. It appears he wrote weeks ago and yet I got the letter only this morning!" She held up the envelope in triumph.

"Please Prissy, you must read it to me at once!" She urged, her mind swirling in anticipation.

"Oh dear, not without my glasses. I'm afraid I rushed over rather quickly and forgot them, so you must read it yourself."

Lily didn't hesitate a moment, she snatched the letter from Aunt Prissy's grip and began to read its contents quickly. Her mouth fell further open with every word. "So, he's okay then? He's alive!" She exclaimed upon finishing the letter.

"It would appear so."

"And he tried to write after all? Oh, my poor Noah, to think he thought I was not answering his letters. How on earth did I never get them?" Lily was in near hysterics.

"I can't tell you dear, but it does seem there was some sort of mix-up. Apparently, he had no knowledge of your move back to Newland and his letters never arrived for you to inform him. Oh dear, it is all so dreadfully confusing, isn't it?"

Lily hugged the letter tight to her chest. "I must have the address and write to him right away, Prissy! I can't believe how long ago this letter was sent. He must be devastated at the lack of response from us both." Then it suddenly dawned on her. "Wait a second, I understand the mix-up on my part but why is it you didn't get this letter until now?"

Aunt Prissy waved her hand in the air dismissively. "Oh, that doesn't matter now. Don't you worry your pretty little head about it. A person can spend their whole life worrying about something that will come to nothing, trust me on that. It doesn't change the circumstance, my dear. What's important is that you write to Noah right away and let him know just where you've been and all that's taken place."

Lily wanted to press her further, but it was no use. Prissy was already halfway out the door. "Buck and I are supposed to be down at the church this afternoon to help prepare for Christmas Eve service. I do hope you'll get your bearings together by tomorrow night and join us."

Lily's mind was reeling and before she could process the last-minute invitation. Aunt Prissy had closed the door and was on her way. It mattered little. She needed to think and think quickly. This news changed everything. Noah was alive! And it appeared he still loved her. Well, at least Lily thought he must, even though he probably found it utterly unforgivable that she didn't reply. *He didn't know. How could he?*

Her thoughts were suddenly interrupted by another knock at the door. This time it was Everett. Lily went to the door, her face flushed. "We need to talk, Everett." She managed to say before Everett could speak.

"What is it? Not having second thoughts, I hope." Everett added half-joking, though his countenance altered at the serious look on her face.

"I'm sorry, Everett. Please forgive me."

"Sorry? For what?"

"I can't go with you," Lily said regretfully, handing him the letter.

He took the envelope from her shaking hands and read it carefully. "I see," he said, handing the letter back. "What are you going to do now?"

"I don't know," Lily replied with pools of tears shimmering in her eyes. "I have to write to him and find out where we stand. I have to Everett. Please say you understand."

"Of course I do. We could never be happy with this standing between us. How did you get the letter?"

"Aunt Prissy came by. Apparently, she just got it herself. She didn't explain why, only that she got word from Noah. Oh, Everett, he's alive and well—at least he was at the time he wrote this. It was all just a big misunderstanding."

Everett did his best to control his reaction for Lily's sake. "So then what happened to the letters he sent you?"

Lily bit her lip and thought a moment when it

suddenly occurred to her. "Papa! He must not have forwarded our mail from Boston. I never considered it, but we left so quickly and he likely didn't want to be followed by the authorities. Oh, if only Mama had been well, she would have figured the whole thing out long before now. I can't believe I didn't realize it sooner, but that must have been what happened. Don't you think?"

Everett nodded dutifully. "That is the only logical explanation. Well, now what? Should I wait until you hear from Noah to find out where we stand? I'm sure the job will wait."

"No Everett, no," Lily insisted. "It wouldn't be right to hold you back from another great opportunity. You must go—go without me. Take this new job and make a good life for yourself."

Everett's emotions were starting to get the best of him now. "What about *us*? My offer still stands if Noah has moved on by now."

Lily hugged Everett tightly then looked into his eyes. "I care for you Everett, I truly do, but I don't think I will be ready to marry another for some time…perhaps never. If there's one thing this letter helped me realize, my heart belongs to only one man. And regardless of what happens, I need to face this on my own. Please say you'll forgive me. I honestly believe this is ultimately what is best for both of us. You will thank me in time, I am sure of it."

Everett let out a deep sigh. He could see by the pleading look on Lily's face that he had no choice but to accept defeat. "If this is truly what you want, I will respect your decision."

"Thank you, it really is," was all Lily needed to say and Everett was gone—into the woods, onto the train, and on his way to a new job and a new life, without Lily Stephens by his side.

CHAPTER THIRTY-ONE

Noah was held at the jailhouse overnight as the station was packed more than usual with arrests from petty crimes and public disturbances as Christmas drew closer. "It's like this every year," one officer relayed to Noah while taking his statement. "People get crazy around the holidays. It's gonnah be a while longah, so sit tight."

Noah was frustrated as he watched the clock carefully. The post office closed early on Fridays and he feared he would not make it in time to find out where Lily and her family had gone. Only twenty-four hours ago he had believed he was moments away from holding his beloved in his arms once again and now felt further torn from her than ever. He paced his cell rapidly, his mind racing with all the possibilities of what may have taken place to cause their loss of communication.

It was another five hours before everything was sorted out and Noah was slated to be released. It was determined that Noah was innocent of any wrongdoing in the altercation with Smitty and his two friends, all three of whom were no strangers to getting in trouble with the law from time to time for similar antics. They were each being held on various charges which Noah realized would make them no less furious with him as they were before, but it would keep them locked up for the time being so he couldn't concern himself with that. His first order of business was to rush to the post office to see if he could make it on time.

It was Christmas Eve and Lily had never felt so alone in her young life. Her father was locked up for his embezzlement crimes, her mother was dead, and Everett had gone on to

Portland with her blessing. As much as she was certain she made the right decision where he was concerned, for the moment it was difficult to face the emptiness of a home once brimming with love and laughter. Her only hope was that somehow she would be able to mail her letter to Noah on Monday and that he would be equally relieved about the mix-up, sympathetic to her plight, and come home to her at the earliest opportunity.

For now, she planned to spend a quiet evening alone. Danny was her greatest concern and making sure his needs were met was all that mattered for the time being. This at least gave her a sense of purpose. She had just begun to go to the kitchen to warm up some milk when a knock came at the door. She opened it to find the snow whirling around Priscilla and Buck who had come to take her to Christmas Eve service with them.

"I don't know if I can," she said, looking down at her plain clothes, stained with Danny's spittle.

"Nonsense girl. No good can come from being cooped up in this little cabin. I won't have it!" Lily couldn't help but laugh at the irony of her words. "You're coming with us and that's final. And you'll be spending Christmas Day at our home as well, that's just how it's gonna be. Noah wouldn't have it any other way."

That final statement was the convincing argument that motivated Lily to pack a small suitcase, wrap little Danny up and head out into the cold, winter night. She put on a dark green frock, pinned her hair up, and touched her cheeks up with a bit of rouge to hide her pale complexion.

Sitting in the candlelit sanctuary brought Lily a surprising amount of comfort in light of an unknown future. The reading from the book of Luke made her think of simpler times in childhood, taking part in humble Christmas plays and singing sweet hymns with her mother and father sitting in the pew on either side of her. Now she sat next to Aunt Prissy who was overly attentive as if to let others know she was not to be pitied or thought hopeless.

After the service had concluded, Flora came bounding over to Lily and hugged her tightly. "I am sorry we should not be sisters, Lily, but I am so glad that you have heard from Noah at last."

Lily embraced the girl in return. "Oh Flora, you will always be like a sister to me. I can never express how grateful I am for your friendship." She then pulled away to face her. "And Everett's too. It wouldn't be right to marry him while I still loved Noah. He really deserves better than that, but I will always be in your debt for the time you were both there for me."

"Oh, nonsense Lily," Flora said flippantly. "That what sisters are for!"

The two laughed through glad tears and Flora quickly changed subject as she excitedly told Lily all about the boy she had mentioned many times, Tobias, who had shown up at her house that very morning with a bouquet of red carnations for Christmas.

"I am certain I have never seen such a fool," she gushed. "Poor, shy Toby standing out in the snow, shivering, and calling to me outside my window. He read part of a lovely poem. He compared me to a summer's day, if you can believe it. Do you know the one? It must mean he likes me a great deal, don't you think?"

Lily smiled. "Yes, it's very romantic. Shakespeare."

"Shakespeare? How like Toby to quote Shakespeare! I must say, he is so very unusual, and a bit awkward, though quite sweet and well-meaning. Still, I don't think another boy in the whole school would have done the same. In books, sure, but not in real life. I suppose most boys know nothing about romance. Yes, I think he might be the best boy in all of Newland. And quite handsome in his way. Surely he would make a good husband."

Flora continued to speak for quite some time of her affections for Tobias, which Lily didn't mind except that she was feeling fatigued and needed to get some rest. Aunt Prissy was still talking to some of the ladies, including Mrs. Thomas, about their next charitable event. Lily noticed for the first time that Ruth was not sitting with Wade. She sat quietly with Leah, who was staring down at the hands in her lap. Wade was with his own parents, walking out of the church and though he tipped his hat at Lily, she noticed he didn't stop to say goodnight to Ruth, who was staring after him as he left.

Flora was hardly done speaking when her parents came over and told her it was time to go. They said a quick, polite "Merry Christmas" to Lily but very little else. She didn't blame them really, certain they were disappointed in her for turning down Everett's proposal at the last minute. It would take time for them to all see this was for the best. She was more grateful than ever for Flora's good attitude about the whole thing and that she hadn't lost her friendship in the process. She gave her one more hug as they exchanged final sentiments for a joyous holiday and the Durgin's left quickly.

After a couple of minutes standing alone and trying to decide a course of action, Lily decided to walk over to where Ruth and Leah were sitting to wish them a Merry Christmas as well. Ruth wore an expression of great surprise at Lily's greeting and returned the sentiment coolly while avoiding direct eye contact.

Lily forgave the tone and decided on another approach. "You know Ruth, in spite of everything that's happened, I do hope we can be friends again someday."

Ruth seemed genuinely taken aback by her generous words. "How? How can you wish to be friends with me again after what I did?"

Lily shook her head. "I understand Ruth, really I do. I know you were disappointed when things didn't work out between you and Noah, but I want you to know I would never intentionally do anything to hurt you. You don't need to worry where Wade is concerned, please believe me."

Ruth was incredulous. "You really surprise me, Lily Stephens," she snapped. "I don't need your pity. It may be over for Wade and me, but don't bother gloating. I don't exactly see Noah here with you either. And the truth is, I don't believe you, and I would do it all over again if I had to, so don't expect an apology."

"An apology for what?" Ruth's bitter words both stung and confused Lily.

"Don't play coy. I am sure Wade was all too eager to fill you in on the whole thing."

"Fill me in on what? You know very well I haven't spoken to Wade since Danny was born."

Ruth merely smirked but before she could explain

Aunt Prissy caught wind of the conversation taking place between the two girls and pulled Lily away. "Christmas Eve is no time for such a discussion. It's time we head for home, Lily, let's go." Lily was confused but Prissy whispered in her ear, "I'll explain everything later." So, Lily complied and left with a final, "goodnight."

Once they settled in at Prissy and Buck's home for the night, Lily sat snuggly by the fire sipping a warm cup of tea, content that Danny was well fed and fast asleep. Aunt Prissy joined her with a cup of tea of her own in hand. "Oh dear, what a lovely service that was, didn't you think?" She began.

Lily was eager to revisit the incident between her and Ruth. "Yes, it was, but please Prissy, tell me what was the meaning of what Ruth said? I have been able to think of little else since we left."

Aunt Prissy sighed deeply. "I had hoped it would come to nothing, but I see I'm going to have to tell you after all." And without missing an opportunity for dramatic flair, Prissy filled Lily in on the sordid tale about what Wade shared with her regarding Ruth's involvement in withholding the letter. He didn't explain her intentions to cause the mix-up as a means of revenge, but it didn't take much for Lily to put the whole story together for herself and realize it had been done to purposely cause issues between her and Noah.

Lily frowned deeply at the thought that someone could be so cruel. "What a mess this has become. My greatest fear is that I will never be able to make this right with Noah. I'm not even sure I'll ever see him again. Oh Prissy, what am I going to do?"

Aunt Prissy remained perky in her tone. "Now don't you fret dear. If there is one thing I am certain of, my Noah loves you. If he can forgive a crazy old woman like me, then he certainly will have no problems forgiving the love of his life once he realizes what happened. I will have none of this worrying on Christmas of all things. You'll see my dear, it will all work out. You just send your letter out come Monday and let the rest take care of itself. In the meantime, you really should get to bed. We both have a big day tomorrow and I have to be up with the dawn to make sure I get all of Mr. Simmons's favorites ready. I trust I can count on you for some assistance?"

Lily managed a smile. "Of course you can. Thank you for everything Prissy. It means a lot to me that you invited Danny and I to join your family for Christmas."

"Think nothing of it, child. You are practically family as it is. Truth be known, I am more concerned about Buck's family. His sister is a bit of a pill and might take to badgering us all with questions, but I'm sure we'll win her over. Just be your usual sunny self and all will be well."

And with that, they both headed off to bed for a full night's rest. Lily's worries would wait, but Christmas wouldn't.

CHAPTER THIRTY-TWO

Christmas Day came and went which included the usual festivities; opening of the gifts, singing around the evergreen, and ended with a big feast in which everyone packed their belly beyond capacity. Lily wasn't able to eat much herself, despite Aunt Prissy's prodding, but she was glad overall to be cared for by loved ones rather than celebrating alone in the blue cottage. Buck's sister had indeed worn them all out with her constant chattering and questions, but in the end, she swore to make Lily her chief cause and referred to her often as "the poor little dear" throughout the day.

After the guests had finally left, Lily was feeling quite worn out from the day. Prissy took the first opportunity to assure her that Buck's sister would not truly be of any concern. "She takes up a new 'chief cause' every day. You needn't worry about that. Buck and I are always here for you. You just come calling any time you need something and be sure we'll take care of you to the best of our ability!"

Lily expressed her gratitude but needed some fresh air and a moment to clear her head.

She stepped outside into the cloudless, chilly night and looked up at the stars. Her breath could be clearly seen amidst the reflection of the moonlight on the snow. She wrapped herself tighter in the knit shawl that Prissy gave her as a gift, as she gazed out toward the south. She wondered what Noah was doing now. It took everything in her not to hop the next train to Florida in search of him. If not for her responsibility to care for Danny, one so very young, she would have done so at the first opportunity, but instead, she would have to wait.

She would go to the post office first thing in the morning and along with sending her letter, would also attempt to get this whole mess straightened out with the forwarding address. For tonight she was just going to focus on the things she could be thankful about. In spite of her father's terrible judgment, the loss of her once vibrant mother, and even Ruth's hurtful deceit, she now had hope things would still work out. She just had to be patient, but it was easier said than done.

Though he rushed the whole way, Noah didn't make it to the Post Office in time after being released from the jailhouse. The snow had slowed him down from getting there before it closed and by the time he arrived the building was dark and no one was around whom he could even beg to speak to. It was going to be a long weekend. He went back to the place he had booked his previous room, but there were no more vacancies due to the holidays. He gathered up his few belongings that they held until his return and went back out into the frosty city to secure another place to stay. He tried several boarding houses, but to no avail.

Weary and directionless, he found himself walking the path of places he and Lily had spent time together a few months previously when the weather was still warm and inviting. Now, there were few people out and about, and he watched with much sadness in his heart as couples walked along, closely huddled together, holding packages from last-minute shopping trips.

He finally came upon Lily's street again and continued walking, wondering to himself why he even bothered to return. She wasn't there, that he knew. He stood outside the brownstone she once called home; the gas lamps lit with the coming of the early evening. He was just about to leave when the man who had taken up residency in place of the Stephens's, Mr. Callahan, came strolling up the doorstep dressed in a wool coat and fedora—it seemed he was coming from a day of work.

"Hi son, may I help you?" He asked.

Noah looked at the man sheepishly. "I'm sorry, I just found myself wandering around the city and ended up back on this street. I'm not really sure why."

"Did you ever find out the whereabouts of your friend?" He further inquired.

"No, I haven't found out a thing, I'm afraid."

"Well, where are you staying? Do you have a room?"

"No, unfortunately, every place I've checked is booked for the holidays. I'm not really sure what I'm going to do until Monday." Noah felt like a vagabond.

"I tell you what, son, why don't come inside and we'll have a talk. My wife will just be getting dinner ready and you can eat with us. Sound good?" The man opened the door and motioned Noah to join him. Noah felt incredibly embarrassed by his current predicament but was glad for the offer just the same.

Mr. Callahan kissed his wife hello then offered Noah a seat while he talked to her in another room. When they re-entered Mrs. Callahan warmly invited Noah to clean up before dinner and offered to take his things to one of their guest rooms.

"Oh no, I didn't mean to impose on your family just before Christmas." He insisted.

"It's no imposition, Noah. My husband told me the whole story and it wouldn't be right to leave you out in the cold on a night like this. It would be our pleasure to let you stay until you are able to figure out where your friend is."

Mr. Callahan chimed in, "Maybe I can help you. I have a contact down at the police station. Perhaps we could find out some information from them in the morning. How does that sound?"

Noah couldn't be happier under the circumstance and thanked the couple profusely for their kindness. A homecooked meal and a warm bed was just what Noah needed. His hosts were more hospitable than he could ever imagine, and he thanked providence for bringing him back to their doorstep. Though he had aged many years in the past few months, Noah was reminded that he was still a young man in need of care and shelter. He slept well in the knowledge that he was being watched over. He couldn't help but wonder if Lily's prayers were at work without her knowing it.

Noah couldn't believe the time when he awoke the next morning. He slept late and wondered if it wouldn't somehow be seen as offensive. He exited his room and the butler directed him to several trays in the dining room with a hot breakfast available for his taking.

Mr. Callahan was still sitting at the table when he entered, reading the paper. "We didn't want to wake you. We thought you might need the rest after your travels." He grinned. "Some good news for you, I contacted my friend at the precinct and he said they are busy down at the station but will look into the Stephens's whereabouts first chance he gets. I'm sure he'll have some information for us soon enough."

Noah couldn't believe his great fortune. The sooner he

found out where Lily was, the better.

The rest of the afternoon was filled with preparation for Christmas Day at the Callahan's. Noah felt like an intruder and did his best to stay out of the family's way, despite their insistence that he should make himself at home. Mr. Callahan had invited him into his library and offered to let him read any book of his choosing. Noah was grateful for the offer and reached for a copy of The Pilgrim's Progress by John Bunyan. He spent most of his time in the study reading by the fireplace, looking up at every footstep he heard in hopes they brought news of Lily and her family.

The hours passed slowly and still no word from the station. Mr. Callahan didn't seem concerned but reassured Noah that it wouldn't long. "I'm sure they are just busier than usual." Noah believed it to be true, but he also feared they might be having trouble tracking them down.

Spending Christmas Eve in Boston was not what Noah had in mind, but he also knew it could be worse. Aside from a great amount of traffic coming into the house, there was plenty of activity outside too. Carolers stopped to sing joyous hymns to the family and Noah wondered how Lily might have enjoyed their surprise visit had she still been living in the regal brownstone. He could picture her now; giddy with delight, hands clasped to her chest as she sang along with each chorus. How near she felt to him in spirit.

A simple supper was prepared of clam chowder, roast chicken and potatoes, saving their appetites for the big Christmas dinner. Afterward, the family and guests gathered in the large sitting room for a bit of wassail and cookies. Mr. Callahan concluded the night with a reading of Robert Louis Stevenson's "A Prayer for Christmas Eve."

> *"Loving Father, help us remember the birth of Jesus, that we may share in the song of the angels, the gladness of the shepherds, and worship of the wise men. Close the door of hate and open the door of love all over the world. Let kindness come with every gift and good desires with every greeting. Deliver us from evil by the blessing which Christ brings, and teach us to be merry with clear hearts. May the Christmas morning make us happy to be thy children, and Christmas evening bring us to our beds with grateful thoughts, forgiving and forgiven, for Jesus' sake. Amen."*

The words penetrated Noah's hearts as he turned his thoughts to the Christ child and of gratitude. Perhaps he might feel merry again soon. There was no news that evening, but the following morning Noah awoke to the sound of Mr. Callahan talking to an officer in the entryway of the brownstone. "Thank you, Nicholas, for all you have done. I'll be sure to tell him right away," were the final words spoken before the door closed.

"Tell me what? Did you find out where the Stephens family is?"

Mr. Callahan pursed his lips. "As a matter of fact, I did. You'll be glad to be informed we know just where they went, but I warn you, it's not all good news."

Noah couldn't wait another moment. "Please tell me, I need to know—and right away!"

"Well," the man paused. "It seems the family left rather hastily, as I told you, but it turns out the father, Mr. Peter Stephens, was wanted by the Boston police for embezzlement at his company. They eventually found the poor chap at a cottage he owned up in Maine. That's where the family still resides, last heard, but as for Peter Stephens, he was arrested, tried, and convicted of the crime so you won't expect to find him there with the rest of the family."

Noah was utterly shocked at the news and stood silent as he processed what was told to him. "Poor Lily!" he groaned. "She would be devastated. She loves her father so. Oh and Mrs. Stephens, due with child. I must leave right away!"

Mr. Callahan was all too supportive in helping Noah prepare for his sudden travels. Once they reached the train station a ticket was purchased for the earliest train to Newland that wouldn't be leaving until late in the afternoon.

"Thank you for all you have done for me, Mr. Callahan, I truly can't express my gratitude enough," Noah exclaimed, shaking the man's hand vigorously.

"Think nothing of it, I am glad to have helped, and with any luck you'll be seeing that girl of yours in no time. Would you like me to wait a while longer with you to make sure you have all you need?"

"No," he replied. "That won't be necessary. Please, get back to your family. It's Christmas after all."

Mr. Callahan didn't argue with Noah but instead gave him a final handshake and wished him well, handing him the book he had begun reading the day before. "You might need it to help pass the time," he said kindly. "Consider it a Christmas gift."

Noah thanked him once again for his generosity and help, then sat on a bench to wait for the train that would take home. He tried to read to pass the time but his thoughts raced in anticipation of seeing his sweet Lily greeting him at the door of the blue cottage in a few short hours. *Home! I'm going home!* He thought with much excitement.

CHAPTER THIRTY-THREE

Lily continued staring at the sky a moment longer when she finally decided it was time to head home. There was no point putting off the inevitable a moment longer. She had to begin making plans for how she would care for her baby brother going forward, without her mother and father to assist her, and it required her to be strong. She went back into the house and told Aunt Prissy that it was time to go. Aunt Prissy tried to insist she stay another night, but Lily had made up her mind.

"I do appreciate all you have done for me these past couple days, Prissy, but I have a lot to get done in the morning, including going to the post office, so I better get back."

"Oh, you young people are always on the move," Prissy replied with exasperation. "Can't settle down for even a moment. Well, I suppose you should do what you must, but let me get Mr. Simmons to accompany you home."

"No, no Prissy," Lily replied, "It's only a short walk and I think I'd rather enjoy going alone. I will come see you in a couple of days."

"Well, if you must, you must. Just be careful out there and watch for wolves. You never know what's lurking in the dark. Are you sure you wish to go alone, my dear?"

Lily reassured her. "Yes, I am sure. I don't recall ever hearing any reports of wolves in these parts, so I'm sure I'll be fine." Aunt Prissy still had a propensity to worry.

Lily gathered up Danny, wrapped him up carefully to ensure he could handle the walk home, then started on her way. The peaceful solitude of the night enveloped her. It wasn't very late, but it got dark so early these days. Lily was guided by the sight of soft glowing candles in the windows of the houses she passed. She inhaled the smell of burning wood in fireplaces as she watched puffs of smoke wafting from the chimney tops throughout town.

She finally came upon the path that led through the

trees to her house. She looked to Birchwood Cottage and wondered if she didn't see smoke coming from its chimney tops as well. *Impossible!* She thought. *Must be the next house over.* And she continued to walk on the path toward home.

The thought of entering the dark, lonely blue cottage left her in a state of melancholy, but it was too late to turn back now. She would have to face the reality of what her life had become, for the sake of Danny if nothing else. She brushed her feet along the snowy path, not noticing the fresh footprints that overlapped her own from the previous day.

She entered the clearing of the little home and saw a male figure curled up at her doorstep, his head hidden in the collar of a coat, hiding his identity. Lily's heart caught in her chest at the sight and she wondered who this stranger might be. Everett? A wandering traveler looking for shelter? The sound of her footsteps brought the figure to life as he looked up and Lily wasn't sure if the night was playing tricks on her or if this was indeed the familiar face of the boy she loved staring back at her.

Noah jumped to his feet and rushed to greet his dear Lily, calling out her name. "Lily! Lily! My love, at last. I've been waiting for you all night!"

At the sound of his voice, she ran to meet him halfway, wishing to put her arms around him, but she couldn't for she was holding her baby brother tightly. Noah stopped short and looked at the baby.

"My darling!" he cried, putting his hands on her arms as a substitute embrace. "What have we here?" He said looking at the little bundle in her arms.

"Noah," she spoke softly, tears of joy gleaming like stars in her eyes. "Is it really you? Are you really here?"

He cupped her face gently. "Yes, yes, I'm here." He reassured her. He kissed her lips then kissed them again. "And I'll never leave your side again. Just tell me you still love me."

"Yes, of course I love you, you and nobody else. Not ever."

He kissed her again and yet again. "Then marry me, Lily, my darling, be my wife."

"Of course, I will! I would be honored," she cried, and he kissed her again. "But wait Noah," she interrupted him before he could go in for another. "There's something you should know." She looked down at her baby brother in her arms.

Noah followed her gaze to the baby boy she held who began fussing from the commotion. "Let's go in out of the cold and you can tell me all about it," he replied, then wrapped his arm around Lily's shoulders and led her into the house,

Lily agreed. "And there is so very much to tell."

"I can imagine," Noah said chuckling. "And I have a few things to share with you as well."

They went inside and stoked a fire. Lily put little Danny to bed and she and Noah stayed up talking about all that had developed in the last few months. It was overwhelming how many misunderstandings had occurred between them. Lily was especially shocked by the news of Noah's father still being alive and what had transpired between them.

"I'm so sorry Noah, that must have been painful beyond words. He doesn't deserve you, he never did," she said, putting a single hand on his cheek and gazing at him compassionately.

Noah too was deeply saddened by both the circumstance surrounding Mr. Stephens's arrest and the sudden loss of Mrs. Stephens.

"You have nothing to fear, Lily, I am going to take care of you. We will get through this together, I promise. My only regret is that I didn't come sooner. I am so sorry you had to face all of this alone. I should have been here."

Lily thought better of telling him about Everett at that moment. It could wait another day. For now, she was too glad of heart to dwell on the pain of the past. "I wish you had been here too," she said regretfully. "I often wished I had not urged you to go, but you're here now and that's all that matters. And I had friends to help me along the way. I am grateful for that, but you couldn't have arrived a moment too soon."

"So, what are we going to do about little Danny over there?" He asked with an affectionate smile.

"Well, he needs a father and a mother. He's really so sweet Noah, I know you would love him."

"If he's a part of you I have no doubt of it. He will never want for anything. And neither will any of our children." He gazed deep in her eyes with sudden longing. They had been apart far too long and the man inside him desired to express his passion freely. "I want to begin our life together right away. I don't think we should put it off one day longer than necessary."

Lily flashed one of her charming smiles. "It might be dangerous to wait," she teased, a part of her spirit already returning to her in the presence of her future husband.

Noah laughed. "I don't doubt it, you little vixen. In fact, you better go off to bed. You need to get your rest for tomorrow."

"What's tomorrow?" She asked, puzzled.

"Our wedding, you little fool. I'm going to talk to Reverend Thomas first thing. Did you think I was kidding?"

Lily giggled in her girlish way. "If there's one thing I

know for certain about you, Noah Sullivan, you can do anything you put your mind to."

EPILOGUE

Noah and Lily were married for six months when Noah entered their newly established art studio in Aunt Prissy's former sitting room. It was just as they dreamed it would be only a year ago. Lily was sitting at her easel working on a pink sunset against a rocky ocean backdrop when he interrupted her concentration. "It came, it finally came!" He announced.

"What are you talking about?" Lily turned to face him.

"You know, the thing I told you about. Apparently, my letters were finally tracked and delivered to us, including the little gift I sent you while visiting Cape May. He handed the envelope to Lily to open. She looked deep inside and pulled out a box that held the sterling silver necklace with the sailboat pendant upon the cresting wave.

"My goodness, it's beautiful!" She exclaimed pulling it out to get a closer look. "You know me so well!"

Noah helped her put the necklace on and then kissed her tenderly on the lips.

"C'mon, I made you a bit of lunch. Let's take it out on the terrace. It's just beautiful outside." The two sat down to eat and looked out at the beautiful seascape before them. Summer was upon them once again and the harsh winter and all its tragedy was behind them.

Noah watched as Lily looked dreamily out to sea as a sailboat drifted by on the horizon. "What are you thinking in that pretty little head of yours?" He asked.

"Oh, just that I wish I could have joined you on your grand adventure. I've never been sailing myself, but I am certain I would love it." She looked down at the pendant resting between her fingers. "I would so very much love to go with you someday."

"I wish you could have been there too. You certainly would have kept me out of trouble. And you would have loved *The Serenade*. In spite of everything, I dare say I miss it too, but someday we'll have a sailboat of our very own and I'll take you anywhere you want to go," he added. "Perhaps when Danny is a little older."

"Oh yeah, well what about this one?" She replied, placing a hand over her growing belly.

"You have a point." He laughed. "Well then, let's not raise our children to be hermits. Let them have their fill of adventure, I say!"

"Here, here!" Lily cried out in return.

The following afternoon Noah went to the market to pick up a few supplies for the new art studio, along with a couple of choice lobsters for dinner. He had just handed his money over to the seafood clerk when a familiar voice called out from the marina.

"Ahoy kid!" Noah couldn't believe his eyes. Before him was *The Serenade* with Conrad standing proudly on deck wearing his captain's hat.

Noah waved back enthusiastically. "My old friend, how have you been?" He called back.

Conrad hopped down off the boat and onto the dock, "It was a long journey without my first mate, but it gave me time to do some soul searching. I come with news. But first things first, how did things go with that sweet gal of yours?"

"Quite well," Noah replied with a broad grin across his face. "Turns out there was a huge mix-up after all. I'll have to tell you all about it—I know how you love a good story. But here's the kicker, we've been married six months now with a little one on the way."

Conrad flashed a broad smile at the news. "No kidding? Well, it sounds like she went and made a man out of you after all. When will I get a chance to meet the Missus?"

Noah laughed. "Right now, if you'd like. I was just getting ready to head home. Care to join me?"

"Sure thing, matey. I'd like to share my news with you both if possible. And it's a real humdinger. Just wait!"

As they walked Noah filled him in on all that transpired while he was away, including Lily's plight and why his letters never reached her. Conrad listened in stunned disbelief at how things finally worked themselves out.

"You're right, that's a doozy of a tale, but I've always said, you are one lucky man, Noah. And I couldn't be happier for you. I hope you will offer the same regards to me in return."

They walked up the path to Birchwood Cottage and Conrad whistled low at the beauty of the place, surrounded with trees, overlooking the sparkling sea and bursting with flowers in the garden Lily had tended to all spring with Aunt Prissy's help.

"Heavens, it's like something out of a storybook,"

Conrad remarked.

"You know my Aunt really must love Lily for she shared her biggest secret of all with her for making the garden a true success. Don't tell anyone, but she uses dead fish for fertilizer." He winked and Conrad chuckled in reply.

They entered the front door and Noah motioned for Conrad to remain hidden in the foyer. Lily emerged from the kitchen to greet her husband. "Hello, my dear," she said placing a loving kiss on his cheek. "Did you find everything you needed at the market?"

"I sure did—and a little something extra," he replied with a twinkle in his eye.

"Oh, what did you go and pick up now? You never cease to amaze me with the things to come across."

"I don't think you'll be too disappointed," he said then called for Conrad to come out.

Lily smiled brightly at the stranger she had heard so much about. "Conrad! What a lovely surprise. It's so nice to finally meet you."

Conrad approached Lily and kissed her hand gallantly. "Likewise, I have heard so much about you and now Noah tells me the excellent news about your marriage and child on the way. Let me be among the many to wish you a hearty congratulations. I am so very happy for you both. And I do hope you'll forgive me for any trouble I got Noah into on our travels."

Lily laughed cheerfully. "Water under the bridge, sir. As a matter of fact, Noah has also told me much about you and what a good friend you really were to him. It seems you played a large part in getting us back together again so as I see it, we'll count all things even."

Conrad bowed playfully in response then Noah offered him a seat. "It seems ol' Conrad has brought us some news."

"Yes, yes," he said excitedly. "Let's get on with it! I'm not sure how much Noah shared with you about my past, but the thing is, I have decided it's time to put all of that behind me. I'm going home."

Noah was astonished. "Really? Well, why come all the way up here then? Louisiana is a long way from Maine."

"I plan to travel by train, my dear boy. You see, I am retiring *The Serenade* and could only leave her in the most capable hands. Would you be willing to take my place as Captain?"

Noah's mouth gaped wide open now. "Are you serious? How can you abandon ship so soon?"

"My sailing days are through. At least for now. If I ever do decide to set sail again, I would like to start anew. *The Serenade* and I have had our share of adventures, but this is where the journey ends. I wish to gift her to you, the son I never had, that is, if you'll accept."

Noah teared up at Conrad's generous offer. Lily too was deeply touched by the loving gesture and her eyes sparkled with tears of her own. "I would be most honored, Conrad. I promise I will take excellent care of her. My wife and children thank you as well."

"No need to thank me further," Conrad said. "You have made me a happy man and I know she will be loved and looked after. And now I must be going. I have a train to catch."

"So soon?" Noah urged. "At least stay for lunch."

"I couldn't. time is short. I'm off to make things right with my family and wish not to waste another moment as there is much to make up for. Who knows, there may be hope for me yet." Conrad stood up and headed toward the door then handed Noah the captain's hat off his head along with an envelope containing the papers to transfer ownership of *The Serenade*. "One last thing," he added. "You'll see my real name is not Conrad. It's Will Barrett. So now you know everything about me. Enjoy your afternoon you two and hopefully, we'll have a chance to meet again someday." And off he was with a wave of his hand.

Noah suspected they may never cross paths again, but

he would always have *The Serenade* to remember his friend and mentor by. And throughout its many voyages, Noah never ceased to say a prayer on Conrad's behalf before setting sail. Noah, Lily, and their children—Daniel, Pepper, and William—created many excellent memories aboard the beloved vessel. And in the winter months, they were content to simply dream of the adventures to come as they admired the painting which hung in the sitting room that their now-famous father masterfully depicted of the beautiful *Serenade.*

Don't miss out on *At Ocean's Door*, the beginning of Noah and Lily's story. Available on Paperback and eBook from Doorway Publishing and other booksellers.

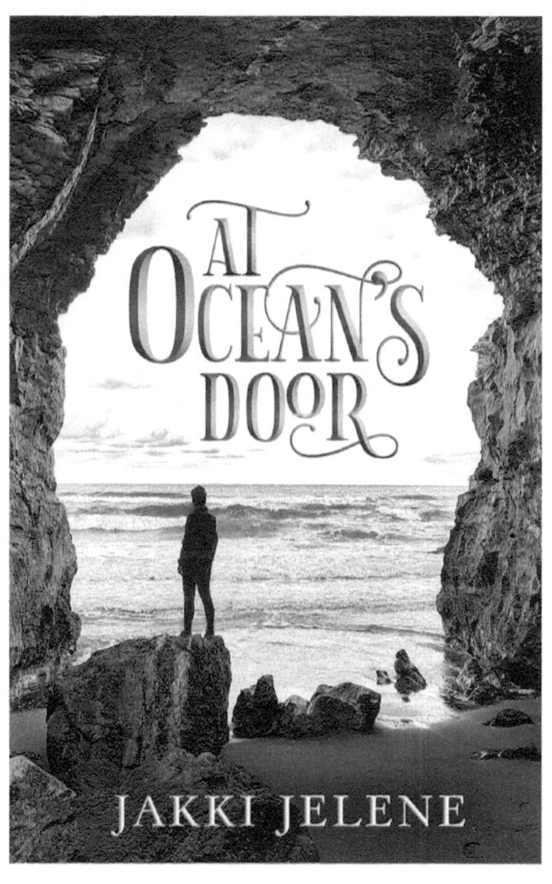

About the Author

Jakki Jelene is a lover of literature and the sea. Whether cozying up with a classic novel or a book of poetry, immersive storytelling has inspired her to express her thoughts in writing for most of her life. Jakki currently resides in beautiful West Michigan with her husband and furry companions.

www.jakkijelene.com

www.ingramcontent.com/pod-product-compliance
Lightning Source LLC
LaVergne TN
LVHW091106080826
845145LV00008B/1826